The Wish

(The Neverland Trilogy)

A. J. Ryver

Ryverland

Ryverland

Vassar, MI

Printed in the United States of America.

For more information visit Ryver's website, or to book an event, contact: X @AJRyverOfficial

Summary: *The Wish* is an original, transformative continuation of J. M. Barrie's *Peter Pan*. Years after the classic tale, a changed and haunted Pan returns to the mainland. Now, he's older, more powerful, and bound by a vow made in grief. As he searches for the newest daughter of Wendy, his lost shadow leads a modern young woman into a world where fantasy and obsession blur. Romantic, atmospheric, and mythic, *The Wish* explores what growing up really costs.

ISBN 979-8-9995228-1-8 (Paperback) / 979-8-9995228-2-5 (Hardcover) / 979-8-9995228-0-1 (eBook)
Library of Congress Control Number: 2025914927

First Edition: June 2025

Contents

Preface

Here, there were no fairies, only angels carved from stone. One by one, the boy searched for the children he once knew and one by one, he found them tucked where he couldn't see them with little stone tablets or crosses above where they lay. Then he came to the last child that he knew, or at least the last one that he could remember. He cried out the child's name and kicked the neglected ground, the way any angry youth would, before sitting down and weeping. The boy hugged his knees and when his sobbing subsided, he looked up into the cold face of a stone woman holding a little stone baby.

The motherly figure loomed over him and the child that he had found, and he hated the woman. He questioned her with wrath in his sniveling voice. He had flown to the same window that he always had, but when his toes met the floor of the room, he was met with nothing. There were no beds, no dollhouses, no nanny dogs, no games, or storybooks and there was certainly no little girl waiting for him for a flight to some fantastical never-never land. It was the stars that led him to the place he was now, but at once, he regretted leaving Neverland. Sneering up at the woman—that child thief—he ripped his dagger from its place by his side and for a short moment, the Devil was in his eyes and the boy made a vow.

"I, Peter Pan, will never let you have the next!"

In such a strong and terrible fever in which the vow was made, Peter's shadow struggled and detached. It flew freely from him and disappeared into the night. Then, his lips quivered, and he cried aloud until he had nothing else to feel. The moonlight was almost replaced by sunlight when he finally knew what he had to do.

Chapter One

In case anyone is confused, the boy in the graveyard was none other than Peter Pan. Every journey begins with a choice and for Peter, this choice was made from a feeling he didn't quite understand. Something about that evening changed the boy—and for only the second time in his known existence, he was afraid. Years had passed since that night, and he remained truest to his vow than any vow-maker before him. He was determined to find the newest daughter of Wendy—"descendant," in mainland terms. To make matters worse, recall that Peter's shadow had left him, too, so Peter was always trying to search for it as well.

The shadow's departure happened because the shadow desired growth and it knew that his passionate vow would be the greatest chance to have it. The shadow found

Wendy's descendant and it stayed with her, using its only power—the dream realm—to influence and align their paths. Each time he fell asleep, dreams about a girl plagued him. She always needed him, but he was always just a little too late to save her. If he had understood it better, he would be grateful to the dreams because they kept him focused and always remembering. Peter would have found her much sooner, but he was angry at the stars—and the stars, except one, were angry at him. Against what the other stars thought, the smallest of the stars in the Milky Way was the one *eventually* to call out to Peter, informing him about where the newest daughter was. This was lucky for Peter who was getting quite discouraged with flying in and out of nursery windows to no prevail.

All children grow up, even for Peter this was becoming true. The boy grew in height, learned the ways of the modern world, and to his surprise and great pleasure, he felt stronger in his magic than ever. He was special and he knew it, never missing an opportunity to make it well known to others, especially when people failed to address him by any name other than "Captain." One day, an older woman tried to get Peter's attention.

"Young man," the old woman had said.

She probably wanted his help with something. After all, Peter was tall and capable-looking, with a very beautiful but often indifferent expression on his face. There was strength and confidence encircling him along with a playfulness that seemed always to do one of two things. First: people might feel compelled to follow him, treat him like a source of something rich and valuable that only a fool would let go. Second: people might feel compelled to run. He was a beautiful thing but was also unstable. Take that old woman, for example. She felt drawn to him, almost as if she innately understood his connection with the Neverland. The old woman tried so hard to gain Peter's attention, this repulsed Peter and to the shock of that poor old woman's heart, he flew away from her with the speed and brightness of a shooting star. With this magic and his beauty, he could easily be mistaken for an angel.

After his escape, smirking the whole way, Peter found a window of a random nursery room. He let himself inside ever so gingerly and checked the beds, but the children nestled beneath the covers were boys. He sighed audibly and that's when he saw a reflection in the room's standing mirror. He adored his new look. Though he always kept his mind on finding Wendy's descendant, he couldn't help but always notice when female eyes were staring. He stepped closer to the mirror, looking deeply into his own eyes and admiring the allure of himself. During his time in the mainland, he learned but was never influenced, grew but could never be grown, and was filled with new desires that could never be satisfied.

He assumed that this dissatisfaction would be mended once his shadow returned. You'll never know how upsetting it is to lose your shadow until you've lost it. The deeper Peter gazed at himself in the mirror, the more suddenly unpleasant he felt. Dread filled him. His head turned sharply to the side; his ear caught by a sound that he hated. It was a wall clock, and it seemed to tick just to mock him. Peter's jaw tightened, and his heart decided to do the same. With watery eyes, he hadn't even bothered to look to see if there were other bedrooms, he fled out the window into the night, desperate to find a way to remove *it*, that forsaken ache in his chest, that would make him cry so bitterly whenever it was felt. It's important to note that Peter cried so often that he always had a slight mournful hue to his eyes. I think this is partly why he turns female heads.

Girls have tried turning his head, but none of them were like Wendy's. It put a terrible fear in Peter that none of them were like her. As he often did upon realizing that he may never find that feeling again, Peter flew to a desolate spot in a city park and cried in a series of groans and wails. This was the precise moment that the smallest star took pity on him. The little star knew that time was running out for Peter. He simply couldn't take much more of the mainland, admit it or not.

"Hurry, Peter!" The smallest of the stars called out after telling him where to find Wendy's newest descendant.

***

Let's now leave Peter to get a peek at Wendy's descendant. To do this, we leave London for a small, American town. You can see a young lady standing on an auditioning stage, singing a song or speaking lines from some musical that she wanted to join. Without looking at her, she sounded like she might be perfect for some theater role, but actually looking at her, it just wasn't something meant to be, and the board of casting associates saw this. After they were done judging her, they told her without hesitation that she lacked the talents they were looking for at that time. It took everything within her to resist storming off the stage in a rage of humiliation.

"Thank you," she said courteously, but her face was covered in shame.

As she walked off of the stage it was easy to see her disappointment. She tried to walk away from the room slowly at first, to get a chance to hear the next auditioner.

"That's enough for today," she could hear one of the associates say almost rudely to the auditioner.

Now she tried very hard to pick up her speed to leave the room, terrified that she would bump into other auditioners who didn't get their turn and would try to catch her and prompt her for hints and tips, all of which she was not in the mood for in the slightest. So, when hasty footsteps approached her from behind, she rolled her eyes, tucked her arms into herself, leaned forward, and walked more violently.

"Allison Joyce. Hey!" she heard her pursuer call out.
Refusing to turn around, Allison pulled her phone out and started to busily scroll, but the pursuer persisted and stopped her by cutting in front.

"Hey, can I give you some advice?" It wasn't an auditioner at all, it was one of the casting associates.

Reluctantly halting, Allison nodded, a part of her wanting to hear what the associate would say and a much larger part of her completely dreading it. The associate wasted no time, her face was soft and sensitive for someone of her job position.

"You were very well rehearsed. I can tell that you work till perfection," she told Allison.

Allison let a short little airy laugh escape her mouth, her eyes darting between the face of the associate and the floor.

"I try hard." She grinned a little.

"Don't," the associate said.

Allison froze and a look of confusion replaced the shame.

"It's the biggest mistake that I see young artists make. They over rehearse."

Allison let another airy little laugh out but this time it was one of disbelief.

"Well, I don't wanna miss any of the lines or tones," Allison said, her face scrunched like she had been told something hurtful.

The associate, still soft and sensitive, tilted her head to one side and smiled a friendly grin. Allison dreaded it but tried to look brave enough to hear the associate out.

"Listen, here's some homework. Go out. With your friends, family, or just listen in on some conversations or interviews online. People, real people, don't get their lines right one hundred percent of the time. Some people stutter, stumble, pause, some even forget what they're going to say, and they have to rephrase. Real people don't perfect what they're going to say before it is said. As for the singing, I just don't feel you enough. You hit the notes, but you don't make me believe in the words."

Allison nodded, biting her lip, and looked like she had just received news of a freshly deceased loved one. The associate saw it and her grin faded a bit.

"Just some advice." the associate said, her words firmer and in a tone that tried to convey truthfulness, "Our job is to make people believe in nonsense and the best way to do that is to make all the little things real. Make me believe, make me care."

Allison tried to take the advice, but she failed to understand the level of depth within that advice. To her, she hit all the right notes and never ever forgot a line. To think that it could be the stuttering girl with too much pitch but a lot of heart who auditioned before her turn that makes the cut—how would that be fair! —it was too much.

Allison shook her head, teeth clenched, the rejection still echoing in her chest. She stood alone for a short moment, staring blankly at the floor as a storm brewed behind her eyes. *How much more perfect can I be?* The thought bit at her, sharp and irritating, enough to make her blink hard, spin on her heel, and march toward the door. The last thing she expected was Billy leaning casually against the brick wall outside, waiting. Their eyes met. He straightened, pushing off the siding like he'd been preparing for this moment.

"How'd it go this time?" he asked, already wearing that irritating, knowing grin.

Allison rolled her eyes. "Don't ask."

"Bad?"

She gave him a warning look.

"If it were good—or even half-decent—I'd look much—"

"Smugger. Less of a sore loser." He finished the sentence for her, like it was supposed to be charming.

She huffed, a noise thick with disgust, and prepared to speed-walk past him. She was *not* in the mood.

"Wait," he said, his voice softening. "What did they say this time?"

Allison stopped, shoulders dropping, knowing he wouldn't let it go.

"They think I'm rigid and over-rehearsed." She crossed her arms, annoyance radiating from her. "Clearly, they don't understand the industry."

Billy shrugged, shifting his weight. His mouth opened like he had something to say but wasn't sure if he should.

"What?" she snapped.

"Nothing," he said, then added after a pause, "It's just… you *do* occasionally overact."

Her eyes opened wide. "I do not."

"I'm just saying." He held up his hands. "They're pros for a reason. Maybe you'd be wise to listen to someone for once."

That last part was quieter. Not meant to hurt—but it stung anyway.

Allison narrowed her eyes. "Aren't you supposed to be with Becky?"

Billy recoiled slightly, hands rising in surrender as he turned to leave.

She watched him go, her stomach twisting. She wished he'd stop coming to her auditions. She wished he'd stop being right.

After Billy was out of sight, she turned in the opposite direction to go home. The whole way, Allison was arguing in her head to such a degree that she almost didn't notice that she had arrived at her door. She paused for a moment, her hand hovering above the doorknob, her eyes flickering in all directions as if she were in a defensive conversation with someone. She was thinking about how to and what to say regarding her bombed audition. After she had worked out a few excuses, she opened the door as if she had just reached it.

"I'm back!" Allison announced.

There was no answer at first, so she sighed with relief. Letting her purse slip from her shoulder, she hung it up on the coat rack, kicked off her shoes, and was about to make her way to the kitchen when her mother decided to answer after all.

"How'd it go, Hun?" was the mother's precise words.

Mrs. Joyce was a wonderfully kind person. She worked hard to support her daughter ever since the unfortunate death of Mr. Joyce whose picture was always kept in at least every other room of the home. As well as being kind, she was also a well-balanced woman—always just enough fun with just enough common sense. She knew when to fight and when to give up, when to imagine and when to face reality. If only Allison had gained such impeccable balance.

Allison sighed heavily but silently and unwillingly turning around to face the direction from which the question came, she gave the shortest answer she could.

"Meh." Allison barely even cared to shrug.

Her mother huffed—her brows knit with sympathetic disappointment. "I'm so sorry," the mother said.

Then Mrs. Joyce shook her head and followed Allison into the kitchen where a jar of chocolate bars waited to be ransacked.

"Did they say why?" Mrs. Joyce said over the crinkling of candy wrappers.

By now, Allison's mouth was already full, and she was taking her time in playing that angle, but chocolate only lasts for so long.

"They already promised the role or something," Allison shrugged fully this time, already peeling away at another piece of candy.

"But you practiced so much!"

"I know that! It just didn't work out," Allison said.

She moved to the cupboard and grabbed a glass. It wasn't that she was thirsty, the action was only meant to be a distraction, a futile attempt to change the subject. It worked, in a way.

"I spoke to a friend of mine today, Alice." Mrs. Joyce cautiously began, "And he knows a nice young man who is looking for a secretary. He's his own boss and doing handsomely."

The "great get a job and finally act like a realistic adult" angle.

"If it were like in the future, I would say 'yeah' to a job, but right now—well there might be another auditioning opportunity soon!"

"I know, but you will still have time for that, Alice. Hun, at some point you need to start thinking about a backup plan. Jobs are hard to come by especially for those who decide not to be college educated."

This made Allison cringe and pull back, not severely, it was just like she had heard it all before and should have known what the conversation was leading to.

"College is dying. Soon businesses are going to find out how worthless those diplomas are. You didn't go to college; Dad didn't go to college," she protested, which caused Mrs. Joyce to frown.

"I know you are just trying to change the subject but let me try to get you to imagine how different life could have been if your father and I had gotten further education… maybe he would still—"

"I know!" Allison interrupted.

Allison knew how the sentence would end, and she didn't want to hear it. She clutched the little cross that hung around her neck. She always did her best to forget, to neatly tuck away the memories where they would be less easy to access but doing so meant not hearing the end of her mother's sentence.

"I don't want to go learn about dumb stuff that I could just as easily and, for free, get from YouTube. It's enough to suck the inner artist out of anyone!"

"Maybe so, but this job will be a sound opportunity," Mrs. Joyce resumed to the former topic. "The business owner's name is Henry. You would like him. He enjoys the theater and is well traveled for his age. His father is very rich."

Allison's mouth dropped and her brows raised the more the words sank in. "Oh my gosh! Are you trying to sell him as a compatible boss or a compatible husband?"

Mrs. Joyce turned quiet; her eyes dug into Allison's. A sudden chill rippled over Allison's skin as she instantly regretted her response and the tone in which it was said.

"What's for dinner?" Allison tried to cover.

Mrs. Joyce had a frown on her face. "Chicken is in the fridge; you can have that. I will be out tonight."

Allison's head rolled to the side as she huffed, "Again?"

The edges of Mrs. Joyce's lips pulled back in a way that was softly sarcastic. "All part of the non-college educated experience."

When Mrs. Joyce was out the door and off to her long hours at the office, Allison sulked to her room and immediately sprinted to the window to open it. It was that time of day when the crickets were out warming up their orchestral skills for the upcoming night. The open window invited a wonderful little breeze into the room that worked to relax its opener. Then, Allison crawled into bed. She lay there on her stomach with her hands folded under her chin and stared at the window just watching the golden sunlight recede from the room and take its place at the tops of all the trees. She rolled onto her back and eyed the ceiling, attempting to count how many animals she could see in the notches and imperfections on the walls, but the number change on her wall clock distracted her.

It was seven forty-five and too early to be so bored. She could sleep, but it wasn't something she was very fond of doing. Remember Peter's shadow had flown away from him so many years ago. Remember that it went on a search separately from Peter and found Allison itself. It stayed in her bedroom and watched her at night. Sometimes, Allison would catch a glimpse of it. She blamed the sightings on a number of things and really, she hated to dwell on it. She told herself each time it occurred that it was because of her overactive imagination, maybe something she ate, or a rare disorder, but it always felt so real. After the witching hour, there it was, looming. No, she didn't want to sleep yet.

Sitting up in one swift movement, Allison snatched her phone and dialed a friend's number. It rang and rang some more until she was almost thinking of hanging up, but then her call was answered.

"Hello!" the friend said.

"Woah, out of breath. Bad time?" Allison hoped that it wasn't. She pinched the skin of the arm that held the phone to her ear.

"Well—"

"I'm just by myself. Mom's working again tonight. Did I mention I didn't get the role?"

"Oh, um. Gimme a minute," the friend said, and shuffling was the only thing heard on the other line. "Okay, sorry. That's a bummer."

"Yeah."

There was a pause.

"Okay, what's wrong. Out with it. I'm not gonna just listen to dead air when I could be out exploding my eardrums," the friend said.

"Oh, you were going out? I can talk later. Actually, it wasn't even important."

"Nah, something's bugging you and if you don't tell me, you'll have me drinking more than I need in order to forget about you and just have fun. Don't do that to me, Al."

"Allison, Allison, Allison! Al sounds like a boy."

"Well, you won't let me call you 'Alice,' Grumpy."

Allison turned to her side and rolled her eyes to the clock, already too many seconds spent on small talk.

"I don't like being associated with someone who falls down rabbit holes."

"Seems right up your alley," the friend laughed. "Alright, so you're a fun killer today. Say what's wrong so you can cheer up already."

Allison sighed. "It got brought up again, Becky. Jobs, marriage; you will never believe what she insinuated."

"I already bet I know. Your mom told you about Henry, right?"

"Yeah, how'd you know?"

"I heard my dad talking to your mom," Becky vocally shrugged. "You know me, I can't pass up good ol' eavesdropping."

"The way it sounded; it sounded like a job promotion with him might include a ring. I just don't want to end up with that real world ideal. You know, the husband, the mortgage, and office job and all that statis quo stuff."

"Well, what's so wrong with that? You'll need something like that someday. I mean, one of us thinks college isn't beneath her." Becky exclaimed.

Allison was about to tell her exactly what was wrong with it, but there was a rattle at her window, which made her lose her thoughts. She passed the noise off as the limb of that old tree father was always supposed to cut down lest it grow too big and knock at the house. Of course, we know what (or shall we say who) the sound really came from; it was Peter Pan. It's best to do a little more explaining about how Peter finally found her.

Thanks are, of course, owed to the little star, but thanks should also be given to Peter's shadow. Just because your shadow leaves you for a while doesn't mean that it completely loses touch. The shadow can experience things then relay that information back to the shadow's owner. Remember the shadow's one power: dreams. The little star gave some direction, but the shadow is what continually pulled at Peter, fueled his unrest and kept him searching to feel whole again. So, now we're here. Peter crouched on one of the limbs of the old tree below the open window, listening and watching whenever she looked away from the window. In one of those moments, he caught a longer glance and felt an eagerness like he had seen her before. When Allison shook her head and regained her breath after the scare, Peter felt like he lost his.

"Nothing's wrong with it, if that's what you're into. I mean, it's not that I wouldn't like it eventually. I just don't want it right now and I certainly would never purposely look for it... I mean, if it were to happen romantically..."

"Like as in adventurously?" Becky provided a verbal eyeroll, "Everything has to be a movie with you."

"What's wrong with wanting adventure?"

Peter did everything to keep from crowing. There was another pause in the girls' conversation. You can imagine the two girls each in their rooms, cliché as ever. Becky waved her hands, pinching her phone between her ear and shoulder because she was busy finishing her nails. Allison switched to her other side but was uncomfortable, so she switched to her stomach instead. Peter ducked again and hid low, grinning, already planning. A part of him wanted to fly into the open window, scoop her up, and fly quickly to Neverland, but he feared her resistance. He stole another peak. He could overpower her easily enough.

"If it's adventure you want, try signing up for a first college semester!" Becky laughed, half rubbing it in Allison's face.

Allison huffed. "I don't find your path very romantic."

"Well, agree to disagree," the friend said, blowing at her nails before continuing. "You know what you need, Grumpy. A night out of the house."

"You mean go to the party?"

"Mm-hmm. It's at Billy's." Becky's voice grew low and seductive.

Allison rolled her eyes. "Oh, great and how did you talk your dad into letting you go to a late-night thing with your Mr. On-Again, Off-Again?"

"Okay, one, we're on-again, so watch what you say about my man." Becky swooned, "Two, I'm an adult. I'll be out from under Dad's roof soon. Us college material girls stop being so *sheltered.*"

Becky's last word dug into Allison's nerves, but she shook it off. Allison's brows lifted and she released a loud "Phew" into the phone. She couldn't imagine not being interrogated daily.

"So, the party's—"

"Going on right now. Last bash before we all start adulting! See you there?" Becky spoke each word quickly, then hung up.

Maybe it wasn't the best idea, but it was sitting alone at home and falling asleep, feeling sorry for herself, or going out to do something to make herself feel at least a little bit more alive. She could try anyway. After all, it wouldn't be right to disappoint Becky—that was Allison's reasoning. Of course, there was a greater reason that she was yet to understand. Peter Pan, though in a rush to return to Neverland, was still never one to pass up a game and this was one of the most important games that he would ever have to win. Peter sneaked peaks at her as she prepared for the party. He played with the idea of taking her now regardless of any refusal on her part. He hated the thought of her struggling against him, defying him even though it would all be for her own good. A flash of her pale skin darting past the window from one side of the room to the next distracted Peter from the thought. He took a moment to let everything sink in. There was something that finally felt right. After all these years, the countless generations, there she was, the one who'd never leave him. He couldn't seem to keep his teeth hidden, he was too delighted to see her, too excited to show her how happy, innocent, and adventurous life could be.

Chapter Two

It took Allison less time than she expected to get ready, and even less to arrive at Billy's—at least, it felt that way with how lost she was in her head. If it wasn't for a weird sound from her car's engine, she probably would have driven right past Billy's. There weren't neighbors around Billy's place for quite a distance, so this gave the party great liberty regarding the music volume. Allison parked her car separately from the line of cars already there. She leaned her full weight against the door to push it open. She was careful to close it though. She brushed rust from her fingers and gave the car one last look of disgust before turning toward the house.

The music blared to drown out any natural sound. House lights were all on and strings of plastic lanterns were strung like Christmas lights all around the border of the party. Her nose crinkled at the overwhelming sound of the crowd. The whole yard—front and back—buzzed with lively, empty chatter. Trendy alternative music, laughter, and noise clashed in a harsh dissonance. She was almost backing up to retreat to her heap of rust to escape the place if it weren't for Becky's shriek.

"No way!" Becky protested, rushing to grab hold of Allison's sleeve. "Don't you dare."

"I just got here," Allison said, stepping toward the house for the second time.

Becky gave her a look that said she was full of it.

"Loosen up, don't embarrass me," Becky said.

Allison rolled her eyes. "Jeese, could the music be anymore obnoxious?"

Becky laughed and winked just in time for Billy to come up behind her and grab her waist.

"Come on!" Billy said. He licked his lips while Becky mouthed the words to the song and soon, they were a modern Cinderella and Prince Charming with a lot less class.

There was something about the host giving his best on the floor that turned the party up, but I suppose with enough booze anything could. Billy Boone was the cool guy with his own place and a rebellious personality for the son of the chief of police. Somehow, it made him all the more desirable.

When the song ended and the two were through congratulating each other on their moves, everyone began spreading out to get new drinks or check their phones or mingle. Allison did none of that. Instead, she sat on a lone patio chair to people-watch. Then, pulling out her phone, she began typing what she observed. There was a guy getting rejected to the right. To the left, there was a girl making a fool of herself. Her typing didn't last long since most everyone was either eating, drinking, dancing, or making total fools of themselves, everyone trying their hardest to *not* look smalltown. All of which would be pointless to record unless she wanted to write a cliché, never-that-cool-in-reality kind of party into one of her stories.

It was ten thirty-five before Becky thought to check in on her friend but finding her wouldn't be easy because Allison had had her fill of the noise and pointlessness of the evening and decided to venture into the woodland at the back of the house.

It was a rather thick woods with lots of bushes that she had to tiptoe through. The party babble was the first thing to fade away, but the music was still like a nagging little thought just loud enough to be annoying. So, Allison walked deeper, ducking under low hanging branches, and parting tall ferns until the music was swallowed up in the moonlit darkness. Now it was only night—crickets conversing, foxes talking. The further she crept, owls screeched, and the racoons moaned. Even the trees were exchanging thoughts. It was like all the creatures of the night were in the deepest form of negotiation. This was because they knew who was up in the treetops looking down on Allison. When Peter Pan's face lit up with mischievous grandeur, the night creatures gossiped in anticipation of what Peter would do.

Peter watched her stumble and trip until she came to rest by a giant tree that lay hallowed out on the forest floor. She brushed off leaf bits and twigs then pressed firmly with both hands against the barky surface to test for durability. With a smile, she hoisted herself onboard and sat so that her feet could freely dangle. Then she squeezed her eyes shut and breathed in like she was trying to inhale every sound, every breeze, and every sensation, like the little white moth tickling her lashes. Turning her phone on again, Allison typed and typed to record everything that she was hearing and feeling. Peter had seen the glowing boxes before and understood that they held information. He wanted desperately to see what she was doing but was too afraid to snap a branch and draw her attention, so Peter remained in quiet frustration.

The trees in these woods, however, liked Peter so they stole glimpses of Allison's phone and whispered: "The girl writes about us and all other creations and oh Peter! she writes about you though she knows not that she does."

So, using tree language, Peter asked the trees to tell him more about what she wrote, and the trees replied with beautiful accuracy. She wrote about a place very far away where people go to always be free and within that place were magical creatures and a boy who always had the greatest adventures. She wrote about a lovely forest garden hidden somewhere in that faraway place where purple flowers grew up as tall as she was. Peter seemed to remember a place on Neverland exactly like that. With each word that the trees shared, Peter's excitement sprouted along with his cockiness. As Peter perched, he watched Allison and adored how alive and adventure-starved her eyes appeared. It gave the clever boy a rather lovely idea.

Suddenly, the woods became quiet—too quiet. The usual choir of birds, even the cracking tree trunks stilled and left only the murmurous breeze occasionally threading through the various types of treetops. The change in atmosphere caught her attention. Putting her phone away, she pushed herself off the hollowed tree and stood straight, scanning the woods. I doubt she could explain why, but she started to explore, searching for the sudden cause of quietness. She stepped more carefully over the tangled roots that rested exposed from weathering as she waded through the ferns that tried so hard to hide them. There was a weight of some unseen presence pricking her senses. Allison wasn't sure how she knew it, but she wasn't alone in those woods.

She spoke softly to herself, something she might do if she feels unsettled.

"Strange…" she said, when a lone frog started chirping from somewhere a little deeper in the woods, past the thicker line of trees.

Then there was a violent shift in the air that wasn't the wind. Her eyes caught a flicker of movement between the trees, practically too effortless to be human, too real to have been imagined. With the woodland's help in masking Peter's sneaking just enough to gain the girl's attention, the boy flew to a small clearing just beyond the thicker line of trees where a log lay beached by the side of a little swamp. The lone frog was joined by others as if they all decided to help Peter lure her. Peter took his position by the log and sat so comfortably there that you might believe he was the log's spirit. Then, the boy drew out pipes and held the little woodwind to his lips. From these pipes came the most luring notes that blended so thoughtfully with the frogs. As Peter played, he hoped that the sweet notes were just mysterious enough to coax the girl. It worked.

Her legs moved towards the sound, ignoring all logic as if the seductive notes were coming from the Pied Piper himself. Rats, children, women—no one is safe if a sound is sweet enough. The breeze pushed against her back and the frogs within the swamp trilled, clucked, and whistled as hard as they could to lead her to Peter.

Allison's mind spun when she found the clearing from which the enchanting sound originated. She saw a man about her age with features that she always admired but never knew that she did. His cheeks were just full enough and his eyes, when they set on her, were luring; they were of the kind that no woman could resist. It was the appearance of firefly flashes growing all around him that evoked a few large tears to trickle down the overwhelmed girl's face. She didn't think about the possibility that her presence was perhaps unwanted. Instead, she crouched down until she was sitting on her feet, and she watched him play, her heart wanting to be his so much that it nearly came up her throat. Peter, of course, noticed and smiled into his pipes seductively.

When his lips parted from the pipes, his eyes studied her most indiscreetly. I suppose he was trying to find Wendy in her or Jane or maybe Margaret and so on. To his delight, Peter did see at least some parts of them within her, but this time it was better because he knew that she would never betray him as the others had.

"Hullo," Peter addressed her, putting his pipes aside.

He stood up and bowed beautifully as he did in the Darling nursery so many years ago. The only difference now is that he no longer has the looks of a goofy boy but the cunning charm of a man, otherworldly, princely, like he was the incarnation of every lovely and dangerous thing in the wild.

"Hey," Allison answered, blinking.

"What's your name," Peter asked, a little put off that she didn't return a bow. It didn't stop him from creeping a bit closer.

"Allison Joyce."

She said her name quietly, lowering her head almost sensing that she did something or failed at doing something, which made her cheeks turn a shameful color.

"Is that all?" Peter winked at her, happy that he would not need to remember anything terribly long.

She nodded and blinked again, which edged a few remaining tears over their borders and down her cheeks. Concern came over his face. He stepped closer and almost reached to brush the dampness on her cheeks away, but she looked him suddenly in the eyes and he froze. Her silence was an oddity to Peter. His hands lowered to his sides at once. He wanted to say something witty to charm her. He remembered it never took long to get a girl to fly with him.

"Did you like my pipes?" Peter asked after he noticed her attention being drawn to the pipes that rested on the log behind him.

Allison straightened her attire and nodded vigorously, which exalted Peter, so he returned to them to play a few quick delightful notes. He had a sweet way of showing off.

"I've never heard them played so beautifully. Where did you learn to play like that?"

"The fairies!" Peter shrugged nonchalantly but his eyes were fierce.

Allison wasn't quite sure what to make of it, but it was the contradicting look in his piercing gaze and his delicate smirk sketched across his lips that drove her to almost believe that he really did learn from fairies. The way that he shrugged and looked down at her was familiar, somehow. It was like she had seen him interacting with others before and always wanted to join but never could, almost like it happened in a dream.

Allison's brows knit, and her eyes looked to the side in concerned thought, a look that likewise concerned Peter. He was suddenly afraid that he had scared off the interest she had shown in him. Cunningly, Peter put his pipes back to his lips and played again, knowing that the sweet sound kept her mind foggy. He was right. Allison leaned into the sound like sun-loving people lean into midsummer rays. It was like a dream, a beautiful fragile vision, just a feeling that at any moment could fade. We've all had that kind of dream where you wonder and hope, nearly praying not to wake. It might seem silly, the reaction, but imagine being a young woman with your head in the clouds, wishing for something that only movies had the magic to grant, then out of nowhere, there it is. Everything you hoped for is in front of you so perfectly, so mysteriously. The cool night air tickling your lungs, nothing but forest, fireflies, and a gorgeous stranger in your sight. A little gasp escaped her lips as a question came into her head.

"Where do you come from?"

Not where do you *live*, she phrased it where do you *come* from because without really knowing, she knew that he wasn't ordinary so he wouldn't come from an ordinary place.

"Second to the right and then straight on till morning," Peter answered.

Allison smiled and laughed a laugh that began with amusement but faded too quickly to grief. Strange flashes of a wild place made her flinch, and she saw the shadow from her room that she tried so desperately to ignore. Worry gripped Peter upon seeing her frightened expression.

"What is it?" he looked at her wide-eyed.

"I don't know."

He felt concerned, his heart was racing but he got up and leaned casually against a standing tree. He crossed his arms, and watched her intently, not speaking. He gave her time to think, maybe come to the same conclusion that he felt. Allison inhaled and looked at him. His presence was something that couldn't possibly belong to the mundanity of her town. There was something so different about him, something just beyond her current comprehension, and yet there was something familiar. A shimmer came to her eyes when they looked directly into his. He stayed leaning against the tree, but he started grinning.

"You feel it, don't you, Allison?"

Her heart raced, she tried not to let it show. "What do you mean?"

His grin broadened as his head tilted to the side. "Me. You feel me," Peter said, amusement twinkling in his eyes.

She took a breath, her mind too flustered to think of a response. She didn't want to admit to anything regarding this feeling, but she couldn't deny what he said. To deny it would be lying, she feared that somehow, the boy would see through it if she did. Allison stood there and kept taking breaths. Peter pushed himself off the tree and took a soft step forward. Instinctively, she stepped back to ensure some distance, unsure if it was from fear or something deeper.

"Don't be afraid," Peter said.

His voice was so gentle it caused her to freeze in place long enough for him to reach her. He collected her right hand. Allison looked at her hand and how Peter held it, the sensation of his warm grasp sending a funny wave of tingles all over her that were strong enough to evoke a new series of tears from her widened eyes.

"I've been watching you," he admitted, closing some distance between them.

"Why?"

Peter paused, considering about telling her but worrying that it might be too much. He laughed, flashing his teeth. "Because you won't be like the others." He stared down at her, a lingering, searching gaze—gentle but stern. "You just don't know it yet."

The words shocked her, she blinked, and her heart picked up pace. There were so many questions and answers that should be demanded. Something about him tugged at her, like a dream half-remembered after a restless night. A truth tearfully out of her reach.

"Who are you?" she uttered, almost to herself.

Peter smirked. There was something behind his expression, something old, unchangeable, and knowing.

"Someone who has been waiting too long for you," he answered.

He was preparing to tighten his hold on her hand and ready to snake his grasp around her waist, but before he could snatch her, intruding lights cut through the trees and with the lights came voices. Allison turned and blinked, as if suddenly broken from whatever trance she had been under. Becky's and Billy's voices rang above the others and soon Billy was first within her sight then Becky. Allison called out to them, identifying her whereabouts. Then, a strange thing happened. Once Billy, Becky, and some others broke into the clearing, Allison was grinning and explained to them that they didn't need to be worried because she was with someone and not hurt or lost. It was then that she felt ashamed of herself for failing to ask one of the most obvious questions. Had she truly shown such poor manners as not to ask his name. When she turned to right her wrong in order to introduce him to her friends, the magical boy was gone. Stunned, she asked her friends if they had seen the boy, but no one had.

"He was just here," she frantically insisted.

Becky grimaced, "You don't need to yell."

"I'm sorry. It's just that—" She tried to explain while looking around but the rest of her sentence got lost.

Becky scanned the woods. Nothing. There were only the regular nightly things around, no nice and imaginative guy. Giving her boyfriend big eyes, Becky's entire manner changed. Her voice lifted into a bright "you are crazy and need immediate help" kind of tone as she tried to humor Allison.

"Billy will look for him, so why don't we get back to the house and get you a nice, warm and very large cup of coffee." Becky fake grinned.

Allison shook her head and looked disgusted. "I'm not drunk! I don't drink. I brought my own water," Allison said.

"Did you go anywhere near that big sparkly bowl with all the pretty reddish liquid in it, Alice?"

Allison stepped backward. "No! and stop calling me that."

"I don't think she's drunk, Becky," Billy interrupted. "Still, I think we should get out of here. Head back to the house, that way you can tell me what this guy was like."

Allison would have liked to stay but with Billy's arms around her, she really had no choice. Her eyes, however, never stopped looking in every possible direction for the chance that the mysterious boy would reappear. The song that he had played was stuck in her head and the more it cycled through her brain, the more familiar it became. If only she could place it, then she would know who that boy was. She would see the dreams and know at last that they were really never dreams at all but true places that had been tucked away until now.

At this point, Peter was more than upset. He was moving above the trees with darkening eyes waiting for Allison to show signs of resistance, waiting for any excuse to steal her, slay all those around her, and leave for the Neverland. She was his to take. For this reason, Peter mimicked that special part of the wind that occasionally speaks to people and through it, Peter gave the girl his name: Peter Pan. It was a name that would change Allison forever.

Chapter Three

Allison spent the rest of the party playing Sherlock Holmes—not that it was much of a party anymore since the music was shut down and nearly everyone sober enough had left to search for her. Nobody could help her. Becky insisted that she was drunk, and Billy only scolded her—his cop's-son side coming out—for venturing into the deeper woods alone. "Did he try to get close to you? Ask for personal information? Try to make you go somewhere else with him?" Those were just a few of the questions he asked. To all of them, Allison defended the boy as if he were an old friend. It was well past the witching hour before she insisted that she needed to go home and get some rest. She needed to sleep, so she wouldn't look like a zombie and stress out her overworked mother. Most of all, Allison really didn't want to explain where she had been. The party was bad enough, but following a beckoning woodwind was just beginning to reveal itself as rather reckless—yet so romantic.

How could she have been so careless. What if he had really been some kind of crazy person? But that music… and those eyes—that beautiful picture—scarred her. She ran it through her mind, over and over again, so she wouldn't forget and suddenly, she was there again. Even when Billy drove her home, she thanked him and said goodnight, though her mind was never fully present. She was instead back in that clearing by the swamp where the fireflies blinked. As she slept, she dreamed of the piper—and lay happily at his feet— swallowed up by the music. When it was sunlight, the name of Peter Pan was her first waking thought.

She got up in bed with such a jerk that she could have sworn the bed jumped a good two inches. Tossing her legs over the side of the bed, she pounced to the floor like a cat getting down from a high place to stalk towards its prey. The clock said it was early, her mother was still sleeping, Allison had to be quiet. Her steps were deliberate. Soon she gathered her laptop from the bedroom desk and with it sneaked back into bed. Her fingers were ready to attack the keyboard as she waited with pursed lips for the screen to turn on. At the first opportunity, she typed the name. She didn't quite know why, maybe a small part did but she wasn't aware. She thought maybe it would make a good character name or maybe it was from some past thing that someone had once told her about. She looked at one link after another, but the results were always about fairies, sprites, and spirits. The closest she came to the name was the Greek god, Pan, who played music from a flute or pipe and kept company with nymphs.

Shaking her head, her computer shut with a clap, but not out of satisfaction. She stared at a wall, completely blank as if trying to remember something that she should clearly know and never once imagined that she'd ever forget. That name! That name kept pulling at something in her innermost. If it hadn't been for hunger pain, she would have wasted the whole morning trying to picture who or what it belonged to.

She dressed and showered and did everything a girl must do to feel human. When she was finished, she had to stand dead center in her room and ponder whether there was something she had forgotten to do. Luckily, her stomach had some brain and reminded her. So began a modern hunter's quest for food. It's not important to stick around to find out what she had. What purpose would that serve but to make you hungry. Instead, let's look outside.

Waiting in his car was Billy. His eyes watched the door with such an expression that you'd think he was some kind of special agent or detective merely casing a suspect's house or maybe protecting a potential victim. Fortunately, it will be the latter in this instance. Billy's eyes perked and he pushed his car door open the moment he saw Allison exit her home. He stalked toward her, shoulders hunched, and hands tucked in his jacket pockets. The look on his face automatically gave her palpitations. What went through her head were her friends, his family, mutual friends' family. Who died, how, and did we know them well enough to be obligated to a funeral.

"What? What's wrong?" Allison said when they met up.

"Shh, half the neighborhood's still asleep. Listen. That guy you saw…" Billy spoke calmly.

"Yeah?"

"I have reason to think he was a total creep, and us coming to find you was the best freaking thing that has happened to you since *The Twilight Saga.*"

"Okay, you don't know that he was a creep," she protested.

"Well, kay, but *yeah* actually…" Billy tried to say in defense.

"I mean, you didn't hear him play." Now Allison got a dreamy, glassy look on her face that turned Billy's heart into an overflowing spring of paranoia.

"Uh, kay I'm fairly certain tooting about on a whistle isn't what keeps a guy from being a perv. Trust me, Allison."

"It wasn't a whistle." Allison frowned, crossing her arms, and gave him a nasty little glare.

He mirrored her stance and was disgusted by her careless response.

"Wow, you're missing the point," Billy said.

"It'd help if you were clearer. Was there a news article or new urban legend that I'm unaware of?" she said, narrowing her eyes.

Billy's brows lifted. "Actually, our neighboring county has been reporting kidnappings that don't end pretty. It's been on the news. But look who I'm talking to, you don't watch the news!" he stretched his shoulders a bit and sighed. "Up till now it's been missing persons, but this morning, Dad got news that their bodies have been found in the woods, all hidden beneath leaf and brush piles. Nearby, there was gasoline and… sorry, the point is, police think it might be some psycho. No one can locate him yet. The whole solid witness thing is iffy."

Billy's eyes instinctively scanned the road and houses.

"So, what, you think I met this potential psycho?"

Billy lifted his shoulder then let them fall back down quite roughly. "Reports show that this suspect is one of those fantasy first, reality second types. The kind who spent his life living vicariously through comics and now, as an adult, found himself wanting to become one." His upper lip lifted with revulsion. "It's funny to me how so many of these types fail to idealize the heroes. Why become the villain? Really, why?"

"How were they killed?" Allison blinked, guiding him away from one of his usual rants that always happened when he faded from party beast to cop's son.

"That's really not— Honestly, Allison," Billy said, trying not to be too disturbed that she'd want to know details.

Allison extended her hands, palms-up. "How am I supposed to stay safe if you won't tell me how?" she said, pulling the corners of her lips into a line.

"I've been telling you! Don't get lured into the woods, alone, and talk to some ambiguous nutjob. If you stay home—!" he said.

Then he flung his hands up in the air and pursed his lips in a *need I say more expression*, but Allison batted her lashes, and his arms fell to his sides again.

Allison fell silent and expressionless. It made Billy wish that maybe he could invest in learning how to not offend her. After all this time, he imagined he'd get it right by now.

He sighed, giving her shoulder a tweak that lasted a second too long. "Look, I just want you to be careful."

"Becky knows you're here, right?" Allison nodded, hinting what the right answer should be, and watched to see if he would be honest.

"Yeah," he replied.

His eyes were softer, and he kept inhaling subtly but let the breaths go to waste like he kept chickening out of saying something other than what was being currently discussed. Allison knew what he wanted to say. He always wanted to talk about it, but all she really wanted was to drop it, forget it.

"I think you should go now," Allison said, hoping he'd take the hint.

"I will," he said. This answer was growing a defensiveness that pushed him back in the direction of his car.

She followed him and was soon leaning down to stare through his open window. It was when he stared back at her that it became apparent without doubt that he wanted to talk about something remaining unsaid between them. Neither would bring it up, they wouldn't dare. She forced a smile.

"Drive careful?" she said, it being a question because she wasn't ever quite sure when the cop's son would disappear.

"For you," Billy said, refusing to return a fake grin, too.

When he drove away, the birds woke up. A robin here and there hopped around the perimeter of almost all the little front yards. Folding her arms over her chest, Allison breathed in the morning air and had to stand there for a couple of moments before she remembered why she had come outside in the first place, but the sight of a passerby reminded her. She wanted to go to a local café to people-watch.

***

It was a short drive away from her house. The café was a nice little place with lights dim enough to fit an early morning appearance with a hint of garden-like aesthetic. Sweet smells mingled together in perfect harmony with the light classical music playlist that the café often played. She tiptoed past a guy who entered at the same time she did and found her favorite table. It was ideal for people-watching.

Pulling a pad and pencil out, because being traditional here was best, she took note after note. She wrote down the descriptions the best she could regarding things like body language and fashion styles then tried to type the subject's personality. It was once her page was full, and she was brushing eraser dust off her workspace that she happened to feel a little chill scattering up her neck and, instinctively, her eyes darted to the other side of the room without her permission. Using her notepad as a cover, she scribbled on a fresh page and watched from the corner of her eye. It was the guy she slipped by earlier. Allison thought for sure that he was watching her, but she could be wrong, after all, it's hard to tell with peripheral vision. Still, it felt creepy but instead of letting it get to her, she embraced her notepaper and wrote the whole feeling down. From those first two times that she had seen him; she knew that he was young and tall and averagely attractive.

Almost completing her notes, movement from the corner of her eye halted her pencil and she paused, looking at her incomplete sentence. The guy had stood up, she was sure of that. It was the moment of truth. Was he to approach her, maybe ask for a date. Maybe he had noticed that she noticed him—was she being the creep. Then again, maybe it was nothing. He would pay his bill and leave, never to be seen again. Allison held her breath, waiting to see which fantasy would come true, but everything got messed up when the door was opened, and Becky came in with scanning eyes. Allison sighed, knowing that she would be interrupted. Sure enough, it happened, and she scampered over to Allison's table.

"Did Billy tell you?" Becky said in a gossip-worthy voice.

"Hm?"

"The killer guy; I just know you met him. Oh my gosh, it's just your luck!" Becky's palms smacked the table.

Allison's eyes were wide like a child seeing something scary for the first time. Then those wide eyes looked at the guy she had been writing about. He was standing and looking straight at her. Allison's lips started to move but nothing came out, and he just walked away and out the door like he suddenly remembered something important. The wide-eyed girl frowned as her sight fell blank on the table.

"Did I just?" Becky said, realization washing over her.

Allison shook her head and closed her notebook. "No, there was nothing to interrupt... I was kinda hoping."

Becky bit her lip. "You know what, I can catch him."

"No! just—just forget it. It's fine."

"I'm not shy!" Becky grinned, getting ready to push herself from the table to retrieve the guy who left.

Allison's face beamed with the reddest shade of humiliation, "No, sit! Really."

Those were the desperate words of a girl that simply could not bear the thought of a friend going on a manhunt just for her… In all actuality, she was fine with just imagining what might have happened had Becky not interrupted. *Safer*, she thought.

Becky settled into her chair, and it was quite apparent that she was filtering through a variety of crazy things to say but could not remember which she would first relay. Allison, however, knew what Becky had come to say from mere intuition and hoped that she would not remember. Allison thumbed through her own thoughts with the intention that maybe she would have a subject that would distract her friend from what she would likely soon remember. But it was no use!

"That's it!" Becky swatted the table. "You just had to have met a psycho. Was he cute?"

"What?"

"Sorry, impulse. I mean, did he look all slasher creepy or like one of those 'you never saw it coming' kinda guys?"

"I don't... I don't know." Allison's face scrunched in discomfort.

"Well, at least Billy and I were there for you. You're lucky to have us."

"Sure," Allison tapped the underside of the table and, strangely, could not help but drift into fantasy.

"I mean, Billy just couldn't stop!"

Allison nodded, then kept nodding at every other little comment that her friend made, switching it up a bit whenever Becky's tone shifted. It was all nonsense to her. They did not see the boy, so they wouldn't know just how insane their notions are. But there was no use in trying to say otherwise. That part of Allison's brain that drifts and daydreams slipped away back to the woods, to the music, to the boy. Each time that she revisited him, his image became more beautiful. So deeply invested in the little daydream, Allison was only shaken from it when Becky nudged her wrist and gave her vicious eyes that scolded her for not paying attention. Allison quickly uttered an apology.

"It's alright," Becky reasoned, quite reluctantly. "I guess after what you've been through, you deserve to be inconsiderate."

Allison's plain little orbs rolled. When her phone vibrated against the table, she grabbed it with a feverish grip and exclaimed an immediate need to leave. It will be our secret that the vibrating was a result of spam emails and nothing urgent at all. Becky's eyes lit up and she stood the same moment Allison stood and, still rambling, followed her to the door. "I really have to go" were the words Allison finally had to say while nearly running away, all to make Becky shut up. Poor Becky! But in all honesty, she really should learn to take a hint. When Allison's babbling friend was good and out of sight, she grinned at her own cleverness and escaped to another hideaway that she knew would be more private.

It was an old church in the woods broken and forgotten since the new one was built in the heart of the little town. It was a cracked-up thing that wheezed in the wind and groaned whenever she stepped up its staircase. Boards were warped and sunshine easily streamed inside onto the empty pews now that there were holes in the stained-glass windows. An old thing, but the sound inside was still something more lovely and otherworldly than any other building when her voice met the tall ceiling. Allison danced around the church, she lifted her voice in a way that made the sun try a little harder to brighten the room, as if jealous. There was true freedom here, no fear of making a mistake and somehow it was easier to be real. It was this beautiful confidence that brought Peter to the roof of the broken place. He had been following her the whole day. Allison was singing about things that made Peter want to drop in and swoop her up in his arms, but this was a structure that Peter would never enter. In fact, he was likely responsible for the many holes in the windows that were previously mentioned. Imagine him almost flying past the old building until the lovely face of an angel bid him to stop. Well, hence why so many of the holes were in place of where heads or wings should be.

To carry her away from this place was what his heart screamed, but he couldn't bear to put a single toe inside the creaky old structure. For now, Peter listened to her songs with great fascination and envisioned how bright and cheerful his treehouse would be with her kept safely inside of it. It was interesting to him, her frustration over things he simply would not care about—things like a squeaky note or an overly wild gesture. It was perfectly perfect to him but to her… well she was most unhappy with everything. She left the church with her shoulders hunched and eyes half-lidded; she even walked in a way that kicked up the greatest amount of dust. It was an unhappy and especially childish scene that had Peter grinning with delight. He followed her home like a ghost careful to keep out of sight.

Chapter Four

Allison had another restless night full of dreams that forced her back to the man playing the pipes. This time, the dream was even lovelier, and once again, she found herself asleep at the beautiful boy's feet. When she twitched and awoke, she rationalized that the dream had been the result of falling asleep in her reading nook, which was really a window seat. The windows, if not already mentioned, were the old-fashioned type—the kind that could be unlatched and swung open like small glass doors to the inside of the room. I think Mrs. Joyce put this type of window in because, deep down no matter how unconscious the decision, she recognized the importance of making a home accessible to Peter Pan.

Allison gazed at the old tree that occasionally tapped the window glass. Her head rested against the wall and imaginary scenes replaced the tree. The little insect climbing the glass—and every other realistic detail—faded away but all returned—with a heavy dose of annoyance—when the alarm clock resumed its usual shouting. Multiple clever ways in which the clock could be murdered filtered through her irked mind, but the same conclusion for each method saved the clock's life: killing the clock means buying a new one, and who on earth wants to re-spend money on something that yells at you every morning. She rubbed her eyes and allowed herself to reflect a moment longer on her dream. She felt grateful that it was about a beautiful boy rather than a dark shadow. Just the thought of that looming shape made her shudder.

When she finally stretched and decided to stand up, she felt strangely different. The room looked the same, except the more carefully she studied the room, she noticed bits of leaves scattered across the floor. The little mess was not from her, she knew that for sure. Her heart raced a little when she also noticed the slightly different tilt of a chair, a necklace in an upside-down position, and the dresser drawer partially open.

Allison pulled the drawer out more and examined the contents, nothing was missing. Because nothing was noticeably gone, she second guessed if she was the one responsible, but that self-doubt quickly faded when she noticed her open notebook. In a large print, a message was scribbled onto the page in the form of a little love note. Now she was frightened. She turned to rush into the hallway to fetch her mother, but then she remembered that she would be long gone to work by now. There was no use in that, so, though she hated to do it, she grabbed her phone and dialed. It rang only three times before a groggy voice answered.

"Billy, someone's been in here," Allison said.

His response was a series of questions and commands with the end result of telling her to go to the neighbor's house to wait because he was on his way over. Allison, of course, just waited by the front door, and when Billy slammed his car door shut and marched toward her, he was in cop mode.

"I told you to wait at the neighbor's," Billy said.

Allison rolled her eyes but hurried inside. "No one's here anymore."

Without looking behind her, Allison led Billy to her room. Billy scanned the place. At the notebook, the leaves, then the window.

"Did you meet anyone since that guy in the woods?" he asked, touching the unlatched window.

"No. And I never lock that. Kinda no need."

He nodded *'yeah, right.'*

"Maybe some of the neighbor kids were just messing around?" Allison suggested.

Billy shook his head. "I think you should start locking your window at night and when you are not at home."

"At least whoever it was didn't kill me." Allison half-grinned.

Again, Billy nodded. Latching the window, he returned to the notebook and picked it up.

"At least he's specific," Billy grimaced, his voice sarcastic.

"That guy at the party is the likely perpetrator."

"You wouldn't think that at all if you had only met him," Allison argued.

Billy shook his head in disbelief at her apparent naivety. "Allison, I swear… When I see my father, I'm sure he'll have one of his people file a report."

"No. People will just end up freaking out. I'd never be allowed out again alone."

"Allison, this *is* something to be freaked out about. Someone was in here," he pointed to the bed, "while you were sleeping. How would you even know if he did anything to you?"

"I wouldn't sleep through anything like that. So…"

"You could have been drugged."

Allison crossed her arms and shook her head.

"If you wanted someone who would just keep this a secret, I don't know why you called me!"

Allison thought about it. It was a reflex really. He used to be easy to call. Billy left the place with the idea that Allison was in unwilling agreement to make the break-in public, but instead of taking being safer serious, she decided to go about her regular routine: driving to the café, writing for a while, then visiting the old church. It was quite late when she finally decided to return home. Unfortunately, the police car at the curb of her street made her wish that she had stayed in the church. It was an unsightly scene that followed. As soon as she opened the door, Allison was met by her frantic mother and a quiet police chief. He was calmer, used to this sort of thing, but his eyes pierced her for her apparent stupidity. The argument that occurred was filled with resentment and harsh things that don't need repeating. It is important to note that the whole scene ended with a single door slam and Allison bawling herself to sleep.

The truth is, she believed that the note was from perhaps the boy in the woods, and she found the whole situation quite romantic, except for the yelling and stuff. She lay in bed, her mind twisting with thoughts that wouldn't shut off or change the subject. In fact, she didn't sleep at all. She sat up all night—fully dressed, jewelry and all. Stewing over the argument, Allison concluded that it was high time to be on her own, to follow her heart. The more she lost herself in thought and embarrassment, the more upset she became. Finally, she stood from her bed with a huff and walked over to her bedroom mirror. She closed her eyes and took some deep breaths, sure that once she looked up, she would see her eyes puffy and reddened. Opening her eyes, she gasped. She looked to the right of her own reflection where a darkness stood darker than the rest of the room, organized in the shape of a man. A sharp pain from fear jolted her body and she whipped around to address the shadow—nothing, it was gone. Her breathing picked up and this newly formed shock made up her mind. She had to stay the rest of the night, but come morning, she would leave for good. She had to do it. Thoughts of that boy overwhelmed her. She had to see him again—

because a part of her wanted to believe he held

the answers… and was truly sewn to her fate.

Chapter Five

It was more than anyone should be expected to handle. Images of his handsome face danced in her head like sugarplums. Every empty part of the house, each cobweb-covered spot in the darkest, least-touched corners all encouraged her to go outside. So, she did. Snatching her jacket and discarding all her jewelry—except for her necklace, Allison outran the few family pictures that warned her not to go. She ripped her car door open, which always seemed to welcome runaway fantasies, and far from the disappointed little house, she drove until she was closer to the woods and the little dirt road that led to Billy's. Of course, Billy's house was not her destination. She stopped short of reaching it and parked the car as close to the wood line as she could—out of sight, out of mind.

She looked up at the trees waving gently from their place in the gray sky. It was hard to say whether the wave was welcoming or not. In the dull glow of an overcast day, everything has the potential for being unwelcoming. She hugged herself and tried to brush away some of the goosebumps. Then came her first mistake, that first step into the woods, which turned into multiple. There was some wind, but then a great stillness. It was her footsteps that became the most dominant sound, that and the occasional crow. She had to reach that place. She could almost hear the echo of electric music fading and being replaced by the sweet sound of that little woodwind pipe. She knew for certain that finding the clearing and the beached log would provide proof of the dreamy boy or fill her with reality. She feared that without the pipes, the night sounds, and the moonglow, she might only find a soggy log and a mosquito-infested swamp—her dreams crushed.

Maybe he was what everyone was telling her. Another part of her brain, the part that she remembered, favored finding proof. But traveling in a wood that was only seen once in the night was more challenging in the daylight. As unfamiliarity heightened, distant frog calls aroused some hope. Bits of sunlight caressed the ferns of the woodland floor. The ferns cuddled Allison's legs, seemingly encouraging her to stay and keep moving forward. The pipe-song played louder in her memory. Wind made the trees wave again and now there was birdsong of some little thrush, and she could have almost sworn that the bird was saying "Pan." Her pace hastened but before she could push a low hanging branch out of her way to reveal the desired clearing, something latched onto her waist. With a dreadful shout, Allison struggled against the grip only to be met by a familiar laugh.

"Playing detective?" Allison sighed and hit his chest with her fists.

Billy grinned. "What else would you expect a cop's son to do?"

"Out getting himself in trouble with questionable girls and thugs. That, or snitching."

Billy's grin brightened but faded just as fast. Allison folded her arms across her chest and looked at him with something in her eyes that made him feel awful. He knew what she was implying about herself.

"You're not questionable, Ally. And I was just trying to protect you."

Billy's fingers stretched to find a comforting place on her shoulder, but she pulled away, leaving nothing but air to caress. She shot him a much harsher look, one that reminded him of their past.

"It was my fault, too, Ally."

Her eyes widened with instant regret for having made the dry joke. "Don't."

"And if I could go back…" Billy said, but Allison's arms tightened against her chest.

"This is why I hate being alone with you," she said, snarling.

"That can change if you'd just try."

She rolled her eyes and ensured that there was space between them. "Seen Becky today?"

"Stop changing the subject." Billy's eyes were narrow now, serious.

"You're not sheriff yet," she retorted.

His expression grew stern. "If I were, you'd be safe in a cell by now. Not out here where you were told not to be."

Allison's eyes lit up with a furious manner. How dare anyone suggest a cage. What she hated most was the suggestion of being locked up and unable to have personal freedom to do whatever. Cages come in all shapes and forms—some are bars and others are warm arms. Both, however, are capable of or even designed to do the same thing—keep you controlled. The more Allison thought about it, the angrier she became. Her face was now radiating enough heat to freak an environmentalist out of his wits. She planned to march off by herself and if he tried to stop her, she would throw the biggest hissy fit in the history of hissy fits, but that's not what fate wanted.

A crunch occurred somewhere on the forest ground and shot through the air, causing Billy's head to flick in the direction of sound. At once his dominant hand gripped Allison's forearm. His eyes scanned the area behind them. Off in the distance, a short distance really, a strange little light flickered then vanished. Allison's mind was theatrical, to be polite, so she thought of several other excuses for the light before she came to the correct conclusion that it was a reflective sort of light. Billy insisted that she walk, but her eyes were fixed on trying to spot the little light again. The small area of her brain that senses danger must have been broken in her.

"What is it?" she said instead of walking.

"Come on," Billy said.

It suddenly frightened her the way she could practically see his heart beating in his wide eyes. The foolish girl should have hastened her walk rather than dragged her feet in confusion. She should have allowed Billy to walk faster even if it meant that she would be leaping to keep up with him dragging her. But she was too much like a distracted little puppy, totally unaware of the concept of urgency. Billy really had no choice. He pushed past some bushes, dragging Allison with him, and stopping beside a thick-limbed tree.

"Climb," he said, looking over his shoulder to scan the area behind him.

"Up there? No!" Allison refused.

Her refusal only earned a rough shove against the rugged bark of the tree.

"Billy!" she yelped.

"Shut up," he said, his face apologetic. "Trust me."

So, Allison was pushed up the tree with Billy about to climb up as well, but fate had another idea. Billy stopped, set his foot back down on the crunchy ground, turned around, and ran away to another clearing almost deliberately making himself visible. Allison almost called out to him to accuse him of playing a silly game. After all, it wouldn't be the first time that he tried to frighten her into reasonable behavior. She peered through the branches, stepping carefully over a particularly gnarled limb to catch a better glimpse of what he was doing. Billy stood still in the clearing, his head flicking to his left like someone had just called him. He was too far now to be clearly heard by Allison, but she swore that he was talking.

Any thought of games faded from her mind when a lanky figure stepped out, hands in his coat pockets, to greet him. His stature and overall body language was familiar, she felt. Now there was a clear conversation and not a good one. Billy's stance was defensive, Allison had seen it many times before. A light little breeze brushed through the tree limbs where she hid, making it more difficult to always have an unobstructed view. There was an unnerving feeling in the pit of Allison's stomach.

She could not believe it really happened. Her hitched breathing almost relaxed when the stranger backed away, but when his head turned in the direction of her tree, she felt her heart in her throat. It happened so quickly. The stranger pushed

Billy, but Billy grabbed him and tried to toss him to the ground. The lanky stranger was strong and fought back. In the struggle, the little reflective light reappeared in the hand of the stranger. This time it was obvious what it was—a switchblade. The attacker raised his armed hand, but Billy tried to block it from coming down on him. It twinkled momentarily from the little bit of light that seeped through the clouds until it disappeared into Billy's ribs. The lanky stranger then retrieved the little light now dimmed by blood. Billy stood there, bleeding through his shirt and Allison, she didn't know what to do. Maybe it was the blood, the panic paired with the overwhelming clapping of leaves that surrounded her or maybe it was some greater force. Regardless of whatever it was, Allison stepped backward, catching her heel on that hazardous limb and she fell.

The tree tried to catch her, but tree limbs tend to do a terrible job at that. The tree knew just how important it was to keep her from hitting the ground, not really because it had any care for the girl, but because it feared the wrath of Peter. In fact, the tree with one loud and terrible crack cried out for Peter and because the wind was particularly fond of Peter that day, it carried him to the falling girl's side just in time. Peter held Allison's unmoving body as close to his own as possible. He flew swiftly away, and the trees were careful to keep their branches out of his path. As Peter looked at the girl's sleeping face, there had never been such a content look in his eyes before.

He held her a bit closer and was prepared to carry her to the Neverland, but a little star that was out early warned him about the blood on her head. Of course, this angered Peter, and he argued with the star that he knew about her injury. He wanted to ignore it, but he knew that if she was really injured too much, she'd be too frail to make the long flight. In grievous reluctance, Peter knew the little star was right, so he flew to the small clearing where the log lay beached by the side of the little swamp. There, on the log, Peter sat comfortably with the sleeping girl cradled in his arms.

Allison's eyes fluttered but closed again and a fresh little trickle of blood pooled around her injury. Frightened, Peter clutched her closer and spoke softly, coaxing her to wake up.

Allison remained unmoving except for the gentle rising and falling of her chest. It was probably in her best interest that she was in such a state because had she spoken, Peter would have viewed her as strong enough for the flight. Her unresponsiveness made it difficult for Peter to keep the tears from spilling down his cheeks onto his lips. He cussed at the little star for being right. He could hardly stand the pain of it. Cautiously, Peter's fingers traced the girl's lips, paying special attention to the corner of her mouth where her hidden kiss was. The longer his fingers traced over it, the more he suddenly desired to have it. He leaned down, so that his hair fell over his eyes and tickled the girl's cheeks. Then, cupping the side of her face opposite the hidden kiss, he nearly allowed his lips to brush over it. The only thing that kept him of greedily stealing her hidden kiss was a soft little groan that came out as "Billy." It confused Peter. Again, the young woman stirred, and the name "Billy" was on her lips.

"Who is Billy?" Peter asked her, but she stilled again.

New frustration formed in Peter's chest. The name had to belong to someone she cared about and so long as she carried about someone here, he would always risk having her desire to leave Neverland. A few new tears fell straight out from his eyes and met the girl's face. The little star that had been so faithful to Peter chose to speak up once more before the other stars could wake up.

"Oh, Peter, the boy by the name of Billy stumbles in the woods trying to find town. And, Peter, I say he is about to be among us soon."

The little star twinkled, referring to the fact that Billy was close to death.

"Then I shall hurry the process!" Peter said, hopeful.

But leaving the girl would be painful for him. He envisioned that maybe it would be worse to leave her. He feared but it felt like he didn't really have a choice. So, he laid the girl next to the log and covered her in fern leaves. He stole one more longing glance at her hidden kiss, then he flew to find Billy to ensure death. But unfortunately for Peter, because the wind was suddenly angry at him, he reached town far too late. Billy was nowhere in sight. He spent the rest of that day, searching for a next-to-death boy until it was night. He did not think about looking at the hospital, if he had, then he would have found that about a half hour into his search, townspeople and officers were flooding into the parking lot. He would have heard that Billy had spoken just prior to surgery that Allison and he had been followed. He would have found out that Billy was there when she fell from the tree. Most importantly, he would have heard about the large search party that soon left town and swarmed the forest like some old-fashioned witch hunt. But Peter, sometimes having a very one-tracked mind, never heard or saw any of it. Instead, he searched for the entirety of what remained of the day. By now, the other stars were out shining in the black sky, and the littlest star could not warn Peter that the girl had woken up.

Allison just lay very still for a while and blinked. She looked up into the night, noting the slowly appearing fireflies. She was afraid to look at her own body, but the reason for the fear was still blurry. In another moment, her mind remembered. She remembered being in tree branches and she remembered the cheery red stains on Billy's shirt, the way he just stood there. Then, she remembered the feeling that someone might get late at night—the kind of feeling that makes you sit up in bed and hold onto the sheets because you just could have sworn that the bed was falling. She remembered a soft voice and equally soft dark eyes. With a deep breath, Allison found the courage to look down at her body, wiggle her toes, and decipher if there was pain. She noted that she was fully clothed but covered in ferns. Seeing another rhythmic pattern of fireflies and hearing a small croak and splash from behind, she pulled herself to her knees and rested against the log, then she clutched her necklace. A few more glances around and she recognized the place as the magical little swamp she sought. Everything felt like a dream slipping into a nightmare she couldn't wake from. She touched the right corner of her mouth and flashes of Peter came to her, but equally as aggressive, so did images of Billy.

Chapter Six

Getting to her feet, stumbling toward Billy's house and out onto the road, felt like one long, slow, blurry journey. Thoughts came slowly and were buried in disbelief. She stumbled onto the road and started walking. It's difficult to describe her state, but there was certainly confusion and a deep need to reach town. It was too bad that Peter could not be warned about this. He might have been able to swoop down, make her feel saved, but instead, Allison was met by a portion of the search party. Flashlights rushed toward her, making her head scream with pain. At once, the rescue volunteers hovered over her with questions. Only when she crippled over with nausea did a selected few of the rescuers ease her to a car and buckle her into a seat. She stared at her dirty hands, noticing the soreness of little cuts across her knuckles and smeared blood, which reminded her of something crucial.

"Where's Billy?" she whispered, but the words came out slurred.

No one said a word even when she tried the same question again. She tried hard to think, but talking in her own head was challenging. In her attempt to replay everything that had happened, she faded in and out of darkness until a sudden stillness woke her up.

***

Bright lights from a parking lot caused her eyes to squeeze shut. Then there were people on her, asking questions, and drawing conclusions about her injuries. This time, she felt pain in her ribs and full-body soreness. She attempted to ask about Billy again, but darkness hushed her. A little sleep later and she woke, blinked, and took the white room into her consciousness. It was a standard little hospital room that needed no description because everyone knows what such a room looks and sounds like. A nurse came in and right behind her was Mrs. Joyce. The mother had old tear paths on her cheeks, and she looked like someone who had just lost a son.

"Honey," Mrs. Joyce gripped Allison's hand. "He wants to see you."

"Billy?" Allison asked. Her mother nodded.

Funny how her mind was clearer now and how she suddenly wished it could all be fuzzy again. She sat up with difficulty. Her mother briefly fussed over her to be careful because of her ribs. Silently, she followed her mother to Billy's room. He lay very still with terrible paleness on his skin. There are no words for that stage of dying—the stillness, the almost-absence. The recurrent beeping of monitors dominated the hospital room. The sound was a cruel reminder that there was little time left. Guilt gripped her, feeling suddenly that she should be the one lying there. His eyes met her own, beckoning and sorrowful. Allison's feet went forward but her heart wanted to beat its way out of her chest and roll away. She sat down beside him softly as if in fear that the slightest movement of the bed could be enough to shatter every bone in his body. The simple words of "I'm sorry, so sorry" just wasn't enough. Allison could not form those words; they were said too much to have any real meaning.

"It's okay." Billy looked her in the eyes as hard as he could.

These simple words caused Allison to entwine her fingers with his own. She pressed her lips together to suppress a sob.

"You're an idiot, you know." Her voice was already strained. She gripped his hand. "You always had to be such a hero."
Billy managed to provide a chuckle that was barely audible—weak. "Never could learn."

For now, his breath was steady but the way his eyelids fluttered frightened Allison.

"Would I at least… have made the old man proud?" he said.

Allison laughed quietly despite feeling like the walls were closing in. She swallowed hard. "You were reckless and stupid…" Her voice softened. "And brave."

Billy watched her. He searched her eyes, waiting to see something in them for him that hadn't been there for a long time.

"You were always worth it," he said, his voice hoarser.

Her throat tightened and her voice trembled. "Billy, I should have tried harder—I should have been there more and really saw you when it mattered."

He took a slow breath. "You were and you did. Not the way I wished… but you did. I don't have regrets."

Her heart ached, and tears slid silently down her cheeks. "You're such a liar."

"Maybe just one." He kept his eyes focused on her, his breath fading but his hand gripped hers back momentarily despite hers beginning to sweat. "I would have liked to see who you'd be someday when everything finally… happens."

She clutched his hand tighter even though his grip started to loosen. "I'll catch you up on everything one day."

Tired, his eyes trailed down to the cross around her neck. "I'll hold you to that." A tear slid down his cheek, his last breath nearing. "I would have liked you to love me," he told her. "I just wish…"

"It's okay, Billy." Leaning in, she placed a tearful kiss on his mouth. "We're okay."

To reminisce about their days was to remember failure and pain. She bowed her head, lifting his hand and pressing his unmoving fingers against her temple. So much would go unsaid, unexpressed. Closure is so often a thing gained only in fiction. If only it had been a fairytale kiss that had power to heal, then his eyes would not have been so frightening and the monotone screech from the hospital monitors would have been cinematic music.

The personnel that rushed in tried to do something but there really is no hope of keeping a soul inside a body when it is called someplace else. Allison closed her fist around her necklace. In all the chaos, she was pushed off to the side and did not notice that Becky was standing behind her in a terribly silent state. Only after the noise faded and personnel began leaving the room did her ears perk to Becky's hushed sobs. Turning to comfort her, she reached and retrieved only air; Becky had already gone away from the room without a word. A moment later, it may have been much longer, Billy's father rushed into the grim room and looked at the bed. The lines on his face were a giveaway that he had already been told of his son's passing, but his eyes were still unbelieving. Grieved and in shock, he asked her if he had said anything.

"He said… he said that he loved you," Allison reassured.

She told Billy's father that she was sorry then left the room before she could hear him crying. It took some convincing to talk Mrs. Joyce into letting her go home rather than spend a night in the hospital. The car ride home was mostly silent. Mrs. Joyce, beside herself in knowing how to respond to her daughter, tried to talk. This was not the moment for scolding or even comfort. When they reached home, Mrs. Joyce helped her quiet daughter out of the car, keeping her hands almost around her in case she needed to suddenly balance her footing. The house was warm with the faint smell of burnt chicken.

"I want you to go straight to sleep, okay?" Mrs. Joyce said.

Allison nodded and was soon going through her usual nighttime routine. No specific thoughts were in her head, even when she lay down and listened to her own breathing. The only thing that occupied her mind was the persistent tapping at the window—that stupid old tree that was meant to be cut down. She could remember her dad saying how it desperately needed to be done. With each tap, she grew angrier until she tossed and turned herself to sleep. But even sleep gave little to no relief because nothing could stop the dreams, which repeated the day's events but added elements of shadows and ghosts.

***

The morning was strange. Coming out of her sleep, it took a while for her to fully remember what happened. Billy was dead. She touched the corner of her mouth, and a glimpse of a beautiful young man was like a strike of lightning but then her memory flashed back to Billy's stance in the woods after the attack. She felt a terrible ache in her chest. She stumbled out of her bedroom to the kitchen and was surprised to be met with muffins and her mother's worried face.

"They were gracious enough to give me the day," Mrs. Joyce explained.

Allison faked a polite smile then sat down, not touching the food given to her. It was too much to process, too unreal. She felt like crying but just couldn't do it. There was silence between them.

"You know I loved him, too." Mrs. Joyce looked at her daughter, hoping that she'd look up. Nothing. "Billy's funeral is soon."

Still Allison stayed quiet. It almost couldn't sink in yet. Her mother resorted to the only topic she felt was neutral enough to get her talking. A mistake, you might be able to feel the eyeroll from Allison.

"Remember that job I told you about. I heard you never did anything about reaching out."

"Rotten timing," Allison declined.

"Real work will do you good," her mother said. Mrs. Joyce really believed in work.

Allison sighed. "I need time."

"I've given you so much time, I don't know when you'll finally face reality."

This is where the eyeroll happens. Allison sat there and shook her head. All she wanted was more patience, more faith, more time. The last thing she wanted was a dumb desk job where you spend the whole day waiting for the next butt to kiss. It's stupid to even have to start thinking about now of all times—after everything that just happened.

"You have got to start facing the facts. You're getting too old for this." Mrs. Joyce prompted. "You need to start thinking about your future."

"I am!"

"Not a future in fantasy. You need a stable life; a job, a husband."

Allison stared at her mother in disbelief. "I just lost my best friend."

"Your best friend." Mrs. Joyce shook her head, grinning out of disappointment. "I met Becky in the hospital. She said you kissed him."

Allison fell silent again, watching a fruit fly try to land on one of the muffins.

"If at some point you feel up to it, call Becky. You better explain it to her."

"There's nothing that needs explaining."

Really there were plenty of things that needed to be explained, but Allison was closed to that deep of conversation around those that she deemed unable to handle it. The rest of her day revolved around bedrest and an unmerciful number of scenes that pecked at her head. Flashbacks of Billy and their short but plagued relationship filled her with grief and resentment or maybe love and anger. Out of everything, his death was the most selfish thing he ever did.

***

When night fell, she dosed off into a dreamworld that returned her to the feet of the beautiful boy. This time, he held the position of ghostly protector, and she knew in her heart that he was responsible for saving her, she just didn't understand how. The next morning seemed more normal. Mrs. Joyce was away at work and the house was quiet. Allison was meant to remain home to rest, but she learns so slowly and when people learn slowly, they tend to ignore rules, always hoping for a different outcome. So, she showered and dressed and left the house in such a rush that her feet barely gave her fingers enough time to shut and lock the front door.

There was a desperate desire to go to her café, to sit quietly and write down all of her frustrations all while around the hustle and bustle of people, the chatter of strangers and the steady quiet of the café regulars always comforted her. Dressed in a hoodie, she seated herself in a more ignored section of the café. She wanted the noise and busyness of the place but had no desire to be bothered. Laying the notebook on the table and resting the tip of her pen on a clean sheet, her words flew all over the page and guided her through one emotion to the next. If not for a shadow appearing over the table and shading her notebook, she might've written the whole day away. Looking up from her unfinished sentence, her muscles stiffened. Becky loomed over her like a gloomy tree that was marked to be cut. Allison greeted her in a simple manner by saying 'hi', but Becky stood over the table, looking at Allison like she were a lifelong enemy on death row.

"I want to ask you something and I want the truth. We're friends, right?" Becky said, pulling out a spare chair and sitting down.

"Yes," Allison said hesitantly.

"How far did you go?"

The question turned Allison's skin to ice, and she developed a dry lump in her throat. "What?"

Becky leaned into the table. "Were you and Billy—"

"Just friends. Nothing more!"

"That's funny cause I have his phone." Becky clicked the side button of the phone and started to scroll. "Okay, I have been friends with a lot of people and friends don't share this type of stuff." Becky half smiled. "I'm not going to waste much time. You're not really worth it. I just wanted to let you know to definitely check my social media networks tonight. I think you'll find the content very interesting."

Allison's head swam and every word and plea that she wanted to make, every excuse remained stuck in her throat. Becky stood, red-eyed, and stared down at her—draining her of every ounce of calm like a vampire. Before Becky got too far from Allison's hearing range, she muttered the last hurtful thing she could think about.

"I wish it was you who died—and I'm going to make sure you wish you had."

Chapter Seven

Allison made it back home just in time. A moment later, and she would've been bawling in public. Terrible thoughts ran through her head. On her way to the bedroom, she stopped by the kitchen cabinet and grabbed a little bottle that rattled when she walked. She sat in her room and stared at her phone, waiting for it to blink. A short while later, she stood up again, lit a match and awakened all the candles in her room. Then, she sat back down on her bed this time, glanced at her oldest candle, then looked back to see if the phone was blinking. Exhausted by tears and lulled by the soft yawns of the flickering candles, she fell asleep and while she slept, she dreamed. She saw the Neverland and could feel flight. Then, there was the boy, and she reached out to him with longing.

Outside of her dream, the window creaked open just a little bit, then was blown wide open. Fingers gripped the sides of the window and in one graceful movement a very lovely boy dropped in. Spotting the restless girl, he grinned with his pearly teeth glistening in the candlelight. He approached the girl and sensed her dreams. Then, his lost shadow passed over him, and he snatched it to have it reunited with him. The moment that reunion happened, Allison stirred because her dream disappeared. She woke up and immediately her eyes met the boy's.

"Peter." She sobbed, remembering.

Sitting up, she reached out to him. Distressed to see her in tears, he climbed into her bed and wrapped his arms around her protectively. After a moment of keeping her close to his chest, he helped her lie back down. Allison rested her head on the pillow so that she could take in more of his facial features.

Hardly being able to stand keeping his lips too far away from her own, he rested his forehead on hers. His dream-come-true familiarity made her grin just a little.

Peter took a relaxed little breath and spoke on a gentle exhale. "Tell me I can keep you."

Allison's grin faded into a soft little sigh and her eyes fluttered shut. His breath was unnaturally sweet and warm against her nose and cheeks. How easily could the whole world be forgotten in his presence. Everything was gone and out of mind; it was just him, as if her dream had bled into reality. When her eyes opened again to stare straight into his, all the memories and stories came rushing back. She could remember being very young and, in a dream, that place between sleep and consciousness, seeing remnants of someone like Peter. More specifically, she could remember the island telling her about Peter and how he used to rule the Neverland and she was always so curious. I suppose this is what inspired the majority of her make-believe games and writing projects. She always knew him even though they never met, and she always had every little feature, the way the corners of his mouth dimpled so beautifully, memorized but didn't quite know it until now. She pulled herself to him so that she could cup the sides of his face.

"Keep me" she said, her breath trembling during an inhale.

Peter's pearly teeth peeked through his lips again and gripped her wrists to pull her from the warm covers. His wonderful plan was to sweep her into his arms and carry her out the window. He had already thought of it earlier and decided he wouldn't teach her to fly because there would be no need, he would carry her when necessary and, at the same time, lower the risk of her ever thinking she could leave him. He almost had his arms secured around her waist and was ready to scoop her legs into his arms as well, but then something awful happened: her phone blinked, alerting Allison of notification after notification. It was heart-gripping to Peter that she managed to wiggle out of his arms and reach the device. Her heart sank, she didn't have to swipe the phone to know what was on it. With tears in her eyes, she looked at the little bottle she had previously obtained, and her thoughts turned dark again—until Peter took her hand. Her mind was blank. He hated her hesitation when he saw it, so he finished scooping her up and he gripped her tightly.

"And we will have a wonderful time together." Peter began walking towards the open window, still there was hesitation in her eyes. Cunning, Peter closed a little more distance between his lips and hers. "I can't bear to be alone anymore." His eyes were sad, and his voice was equally grieved.

That was the magic phrase, she clutched him and wept. "Peter, I wish with all my heart that I could feel right again."

Home was no longer home, there were too many mistakes and things that the people in this small town could never understand. To stay would be lonely but to leave would be freedom. Peter held the girl closer and stepped up onto the windowsill as if his feet had wings. The breeze washed over them both, pushing their hair into whimsical patterns and attempting to dry any tear stains on the girl's face. For Peter, the next step meant total triumph. He thought back, though he had tried suppressing it, to the night in the cemetery and the look on that stone woman's face. When he recalled his vow, a devilish grin lifted the sweet corners of his lovely mouth. A reflection in the window caught his attention, he still saw so clearly the spirit of a boy. He thought himself quite clever and with that final thought he soared into the darkness and into the woods, or more specifically, just above the shadowy treetops.

Now the way to Neverland is complicated. He would say to so many young people that it is located second to the right and straight on till morning, but in truth these instructions are completely meaningless and only Peter really understood the way—him and the fairies, actually. One thing is for certain, it was an awfully long trip. Allison was mostly stuck in a dazed little state where she almost believed that she was dreaming. Sometimes, she would swear that she could hear waves and sea birds. Sometimes she felt the need to snuggle closer to the warmth that held her because of the cold and other times she would feel far too warm. Sometimes she felt hungry and sometimes she didn't. It's so difficult to explain the trip because it's difficult to explain Allison's condition and even more difficult to explain Peter's. One thing is for certain, these feelings that Allison had were what eventually caused her fully to awake and take in her surroundings and situation for the first time. There was water and there were seagulls. It was warm and her stomach was growling. She licked her lips to give her voice enough courage to speak, but it took several attempts to say anything because she thought she was dead. You see there is so much confusion about who or what Peter Pan is, anyone who knows his name would likely have their own two cents to toss at you. For example, generations ago, I think it was Wendy's mother who believed Peter to be some form of spirit. Perhaps some of this logic now lingers in Allison.

"I don't remember how I died," the girl finally said but choked on the words a little.

She clung all the tighter to him and this talk of death confused Peter. He narrowed his brows and grinned to the side.

"You didn't die; I saved you from it." Peter smiled a bit brighter like a wonderful hero would.

She sniffled, cleared her throat and wiped her eyes. She was quiet for a while and thought that maybe she was dreaming. She remembered picking up the bottle and the phone, but she didn't have any of the objects on her person. Perhaps she had taken the pills, and all of this was the result of a coma. Peter's hold tightened partly for her reassurance but mostly out of a selfish warning that he would never let her go. Somehow, even in his hold, Allison still questioned her state. If she were close to fatally unconscious, she suddenly felt sad and horrified that someone might give up on waiting for her to wake up and the dream would end.

Chapter Eight

Flying to Neverland this time felt strange for Peter. It would be the first time that he would carry his guest all the way, which sometimes made snatching food from the birds very difficult, but on this new day, at least, Allison was coming around. In the first days of the flight, she clung to him as if at any moment he would let his arms fall to his sides, but now she would laugh and allow her hands to tease the wind.

She thought occasionally of home but not much because, in her heart, she still believed that it was one big dream, so she wanted to enjoy the ride whenever she suddenly felt less terrified to do so. The dreamy feeling only worsened when Peter took her closer to the ocean's surface to see a dolphin pod so that she could touch each of them on the fins. After she mistakenly touched a shark, she made such an awful fuss so that Peter was obligated to shoot back up into the clouds. By this time, yet another moon kissed the sky, and to calm her, Peter lay flat on the wind allowing her to sleep on top of him. This had turned into a favorite thing to do because he loved the way she would hug him tightly. She slept so sweetly against him that when it came time to get off the wind to enter the atmosphere of the Neverland, he gathered her in his arms and flew toward the island, still untouched by sunlight.

Need I remind you that this island was a nightmarish place to be when the sun was still asleep. Peter flew low enough to feel the treetops brush against his feet. Something invisible pushed against him, making him fight to move forward rather than hang in the air like a fly caught in a web. These forces would even tug at him until his sparkling eyes stared into a place not visible to anyone untrained to see it.

Then he would listen for a while and whatever he heard made him cradle the sleeping girl even closer to his chest, then he went on to land among the tree branches that held his treehouse. This little house in the trees had been extended and built upon so that it was very roomy and cozy.

There was a rustic little dining room, complete with dishes and many of the little things that make a dining room a dining room. There was also a lovely balcony, complete with a swing large enough to fit two, which was hung off a thick branch. To swing on it, one would have to fly to it or balance on the branch and lower oneself onto the swing. Getting down or up from it would be a problem if flying isn't a strong suit. A bedroom was also included. In this room, there was a vanity with a mirror, a bed with bear skins on it and other soft coverings, and lots of little treasures that he knew a girl would love.

The bedroom was the first place he took the girl. He laid her on the bed and when she shivered a little, he covered her at once. Then he did something a bit peculiar. He sat at the end of the bed and watched her until beams of sunlight sneaked into the room and tickled their eyelashes. Birds began singing and because the island could sense Peter's long-awaited return, the whole of Neverland was bursting with new life. The natives of Neverland woke up and celebrated his return with a ritual. You could tell by the smoke that danced in a variety of shapes and sizes off in the distance so that they look like strange clouds that could swim and dart in the sky. Fairies, too, flew to the bedroom's open walls and perched to watch the couple, their little lights dressed the room to the point of giving the place a whimsy style. Allison's eyes fluttered and opened slowly then she looked at the boy at the end of the bed. He grinned at her, and she grinned back dreamily.

"Are you hungry?" Peter asked, offering her some fruit that he happened to pluck on their way into the treehouse.

Allison sat up in bed and reached out to accept it. Looking up from the first juicy bite, she noticed the fairies kicking their legs and chattering in fairy language. Again, her eyes found Peter's, which were watching her with curiosity. I guess she still felt like it was a dream. Suddenly his curiosity turned to concern so he carefully crawled closer to her and with one hand, he gently wiped juice from the corner of her lips and with the other hand he pushed some hair away from her eyes. This made her feel compelled to talk things out.

"I'm sorry for not talking much." She felt like an apology was the best thing to say first. "Believing… it's just hard.

I guess I'm still waiting for everything to fade to darkness."

"Allison, you'll find that the sun always comes up here. See the blue skies and how fresh and green the forest is. And feel that breeze?" Peter closed his eyes and inhaled.

Allison did look at everything that Peter referenced and on cue, she closed her eyes to feel the wind peck her cheeks but just as quickly as the whole scene filled her with wonder, logic expelled the beauty.

"If this is real, my family and everyone—what are they thinking right now. How long has it been?" She crossed her arms insecurely.

Peter crossed his arms, too, but out of triumph because there really isn't much about him that's insecure. "Long enough," he said, feeling pleased with himself for finally having her here.

His tone flew over her head. Now she just stared at her knees and spoke out loud but quiet to herself.

"They hate me now for sure and they'll hate me even more for having run away. Perhaps they think I'm dead. And if none of this is real, which is the more probable answer, then I must be next to death in a grotesquely white room," she whispered. "I bet the doctors are trying to convince my mother right now that she should let me go."

Allison had slipped off the bed and was standing near the vanity, which was occupied by a few fairies who were waiting intently to see if Peter would win. Peter lifted from the bed, hovering just above the floor, and he drifted to her side then allowed his feet to set back down so that he stood close behind her. He brushed her hair over to one side of her neck and rested his chin on the exposed side to stare at the both of them in the mirror.

"The past is nothing to you now." Peter's eyes sparkled. "You'll forget them all soon. I promise."

"Forget?" she turned to face him. "Forgetting is just as realistic as believing in this dream. What have I done?"

Peter tensed. She had been so miserable! He saved her, took her away from everything but now she complains. Even worse, she disbelieves in the island—in him. His brows knit together; his expression hurt when he encouraged her to look at him. Grabbing her hand, he dragged her toward the balcony and regardless of her resistance, he managed to lift her so that they would float together as soon as he stepped off the deck. With them came a small cloud of fairies who circled around then dispersed to the bushes and twigs and behind tufts of grass once Peter's feet touched the lush ground. "How shall I prove this to you?" It was a question but not really. He still held her tightly.

It took a little thinking, but soon he had an idea. Putting her back on her own feet, he pressed her to a particularly soft part of the ground. He motioned for her to lie back into the tall soft grass and mossy pillows. Then, with a sly grin, he soared up into the nearest tree like a bird and leaned on a branch. She watched him dangle one leg off the branch like he wasn't remotely afraid to fall. His flute was now positioned in front of his lips and as soon as he breathed life into it, she was enlightened. Remarkable how real beautiful things can seem when you're properly reminded of the impossible. Familiar tears visited her eyes again just like they did when she heard him play the first time. She lay there unbothered because nothing was imperfect. Fading between sleep and that fully awake state, she smiled every time some naughty little fairy tugged at Peter's hair.

Describing the power that the Neverland has over memory is an impossible task. I don't think anyone really understands how this island works, but some guesses might be the magic of stubbornness and longing. This place feeds on these emotions, I think. This is how forgetting about loved ones and responsibility is achieved and even justified— they simply have no lasting place here where dreams and adventure take precedence. One short nap later, and Allison was more vulnerable to believing both in Neverland and in him. Upon waking, she looked back up at the boy and fell in love with how rhythmically he swung his leg back and forth, lulling her to keep resting her eyes again.

Allison's eyes were half lidded.

"You know… they call you a spirit. A symbol of stubborn youth," she murmured, not really knowing where she got this information.

Her head fell back to spy up into the trees where he perched. Birds chirped happily, some cuckooing occasionally, almost in harmony with the babbling spring that flowed somewhere nearby. Peter thought about what she said, then ceased to play. His eyes stared down at her, big but soft and full of mischievous delight. He came to her down from the tree branch, ducking under the leaf adorned twigs that got in the way of his face. Each careful step was like an angel's in her eyes, and it made her once again question whether the scene was truly real. His toes touched the ankle high grass, and he walked to her, never once letting his heels touch the ground. He almost always half flies. He peered down at her through his dark lashes, his tongue darting out to moisten his lips as he reached out to take her hand. Pulling her to her feet and closer to him, he gingerly placed her nervous fingers against his chest. She inhaled sharply; a bit lightheaded from the motion. He gave her a moment to react, to feel the warmth of his skin, the motion of his rising and falling chest. The strands of her hair moved in his breath as he closed some additional distance between them. She concentrated and he fought to hide a laugh as he desperately wanted to keep the moment serious. A sparkle returned to his eyes again, his breath sweet against her face as he spoke.

"Do I feel like a spirit to you?"

Chapter Nine

In the days to follow Peter and Allison spent most of their time around the treehouse and the surrounding woods. They would talk and talk some more and when they were not talking about this and that, Peter would play his pipes, and Allison would fall in and out of beautiful daydreams. Each morning would begin with a new fruit to try and a bath in the nearby spring. The playfulness here was something unfathomable as can be observed during one such bath. The way they would splash and play in the water would bring you to mind of how easy everything can be when you just let go. It is important to note that Peter was right in saying that Allison would soon forget about the people of her past. Neverland has a spectacular way of making people feel as if they had always been, and somehow you come to know yourself better in a few days covered in the island's air than a hundred years in the smog of the "real" world—commonly referred to as the "mainland" in Neverland slang.

Birds in this place are beyond description; they make music that would bring nothing but shame to the sweetest nightingale or any other mainland-bound fowl. Quite often, Peter would take her into the trees to see the birds then show off how well he could mimic them—he is the only one who could do a better job than they, but eventually he would tire of the sound and bring his pipes to his lips instead. He believed he was more beautiful anyway.

"I don't believe I've ever heard the pipes played the way you do, Peter." Allison would say.

At this, Peter would feel very proud, so much so that he'd take her hand and guide her through the treetops. It would always be so happy, and she'd smile so much—until she'd frown, a natural reaction to Peter's sudden, unpredictable moods. Peter always became so still and quiet when the evening sneaked into the trees. It's not that he would be any less playful, of course, he would just become more thoughtful, frightfully thoughtful, and there would always be an unnerving glint in his eyes.

He would never allow Allison to remain outside during this time of day, nor would he let her be out during the night. He would ask her nicely to come inside, but if she ever resisted, he would take her by the arm, then pick her up to carry her back to the safety of the treehouse. They would spend the rest of the night talking quietly to each other, but Peter would be distracted by strange coos and distant calls in the night, causing him to stare into the darkness below the deck of the balcony rather than truly listen to Allison.

She noticed his angry expression and the way his fingers twitched into tight fists. He didn't want to worry her. He thought that maybe the strange sounds and shapes in the darkness were some vagabond pirates or some wicked force. Peter wanted to go immediately into the night and face these elusive things, but then how could he ensure that Allison would stay inside the treehouse. She might try to climb down. He turned his back to the outside and crept into the room. At this point, Allison had already gone to bed and was already beginning to doze. Sitting down next to her, he reached out nearly to touch her hidden kiss.

Leaving her during the day also seemed bad. It seemed to him that the only way to satisfy both desires was to take her deeper into the forest to explore the situation together, if there were still pirates out there, then he could kill them easily and still keep a watchful eye on Allison. With this plan in his head, he curled up next to Allison and rested his head. Rarely was he burdened by too deep of thoughts but tonight was different. A feeling lingered over him—something like fear, a feeling he hoped he would've lost—which made him wrap an arm around the girl, afraid she would leave him one day. He held her closer and felt her ribs expand and shrink.

Morning crept into the bedroom, and Allison was the first to wake. Peter slept so softly that she couldn't bear the thought of waking him. Slipping out from the covers, she grabbed some fresh clothes and tiptoed to the balcony where she tied a rope in the style of a mountain climber to descend. She threw her leg over and secured herself. Ready to begin her descension, her eyes darted to a flash of fingers that grabbed her sleeve then into a pair of wide eyes, drenched in betrayal.

"Peter, you're awake," Allison said— too brightly.

Of course, she didn't intentionally mean to do anything wrong. It was morning and there was light everywhere, and there was no rule forbidding her from being out of his sight during daytime. She had nothing to feel guilty about, but somehow, she couldn't keep her eyes locked on his for too long, which only made her look blameworthy in Peter's view. In his silent anger at her disobedience for his unspoken rule, old savage thoughts pulled at his memory, and he remembered various punishments he could provide. When these specifics came back to him, suddenly he remembered the lost boys.

If it were any of the lost boys disobeying him, he would have had starved them or took them into battle, only to turn against them, among other things, but he couldn't quite think about how to handle a girl and besides, her escape attempt did help him remember the lost boys, saving him from the embarrassment of not remembering. This helped to calm him though he didn't show it well.

"Yes, I'm awake." Peter gnashed his teeth at her.

Allison frowned and pulled herself back onto the deck. "I'm sorry, Peter." She touched his upper arm. "I didn't mean to scare you."

Peter jerked away from her, clearly offended. "I just didn't want you to fall."

"You could teach me how to fly," she said almost shyly. But the suggestion was like death to Peter's ears so he came up with the first excuse that he could think about.

"Not now, I wanted to introduce you to the lost boys." He smiled fleetingly.

"Who are the lost boys?"

Allison's eyes lit up excitedly, but Peter knew that he had somehow trapped himself in a dangerous situation. Still, he kept a smile on his face. He had to think a moment about how to answer her question because although he remembered about them, he still had a hard time recalling any specifics.

"My crew…" He smiled a little.

"Crew?"

He nodded then extended his hand. "Shall we get dressed?"

"I'd like to freshen up first," she agreed.

"You know," Peter raised a brow, "we could go to the seashore, and I could show you Mermaid Lagoon. I do think you would enjoy it."

Allison grinned. "I think it's best that you introduce me to the fellow islanders," she shook her head, then it dawned on her. "Peter? What are they like? Will they like me?"

Peter didn't know. It was only recently that he even remembered that there were others on the island. He shrugged with a playful smirk, masking his blank memory with humor. Allison made a humming noise. An emotionally intelligent person would have heard the insult in the noise she made. It's not, of course, that Peter was emotionally unintelligent, it's just that his mind was on the lost boys. He tried desperately to remember them, even just one of them in detail, but it seemed pointless. For once, he felt overwhelmed by his lack of memory. It was really Allison who was more emotionally unintelligent or maybe just too distracted to notice his discomfort.

But this is part of his charm and effect—he has a shield and he uses it well. Until you've been lured by Peter and have been face-to-face with him, you can't quite imagine how persuasive his charm is and how easily he can make you see him the way he wants you to see him. All the red flags blur into an evening sky and the danger is so easily disfigured and transformed into something sweet and fun. This is what happened today. They flew to their spring and the clothes, except for undergarments, came off as soon as they touched the ground. They splashed and played while they bathed. It was usually Peter who started it even after Allison insisted that they had no time for it today, but he was especially determined to be as distracting as possible. While they were sitting together in the middle of the spring, he had pulled her against him quite suddenly and started to tell her about how many fairy lovers had used the banks of the spring for their ceremonies. It was dreadfully romantic the way he spoke about it—it made her heart race. He smiled down at her.

"Allison," he whispered, leaning so close his lips nearly brushed her ear, "I think I know something we could do."

She felt her whole-body blush and all she could do was go completely silent, making Peter wonder what he had done. She turned momentarily away from him to regain her footing and stand up, all the while her imagination wandered. The deeper the thoughts became, the more the situation became intriguing. She was out of the water by now. When she met his eyes, self-awareness crept back to her, how her garments clung to her, making her want to hide behind the low-hanging branches for more coverage. Peter, still sitting in the spring, watched her in complete puzzlement. Their minds were fluttering around the same topic. This is the danger of having feelings, they make your mind a total blur and cloud the senses. Had they been able to take their eyes from each other, then they might have noticed the shadowy figures watching them just over there in those bushes and there behind that line of trees.

Chapter Ten

There were twenty of them in total, not counting two who always tried to avoid confrontation whenever possible or feasible. Most, except for their leader, wore animal skins with the head of the slain beast as a hood—one that could be raised or left to hang down their backs. They could move through the trees and bushes just as swiftly and cunningly as the beasts that they wore. For an unsuspecting visitor, stumbling across the path of any one of these boys might lead you to believe you were in the way of a real wolf or bear. Many of them had a prey drive in their eyes that was almost feral. Every moment or every other moment, they would look to their master for approval. They had their spears and arrows ready for striking and stabbing, nearly salivating and twitching for the chance to lunge at the couple. It's hard to tell when these boys came to

Neverland, but one thing was for certain, they did not recognize Peter.

Speaking of Peter, he had given up hope that Allison would return to the water so he, too, was on dry ground to dress. It was a good thing that they had chosen to do so because it made them appear slightly more human to the hunters that were still waiting to strike. When Allison had covered herself with dry clothes, she shyly returned to Peter to apologize. She had just made it into his arms and was gazing into his playful eyes when a small sound caught Peter's attention. Swift as a startled fowl, he grabbed her and shot upward into the sky before the first dart could hit them. Had it not been for Peter's keen hearing, Allison would have been choking on her own poisoned blood by now. Oh, but flying did give them an advantage, yet made things a little more hazardous.

Lost boys began leaving their posts and appearing in the clearing where they could aim their weapons into the air. Peter, however, was skilled at this game, instincts can never be forgotten, so he managed to outmaneuver their attempts. Peter flew away, placing Allison in a tree at the other side of the spring. She begged him not to return to the clearing, but he had a look on his face that she hadn't known before. She attempted to open her mouth again to protest, but he made stern eye contact, which caused the words to stick in her throat. He returned to the clearing with one thing in mind.

He could attack much like an eagle, picking one boy up and flying a distance into the sky before letting the boy fall. Then, out of total thrill for his own power, Peter hovered in the air, arms outstretched, daring the next to strike. The lost boys were frantically running around like field mice in Peter's view, and he could tell that they were talking about him, trying to figure out what or who he was.

"I am your captain!" He taunted. "Why do you not cheer for my return?"

Now the lost boys were cowering, and a silence fell upon them, then there were whispers and old stories quickly shared among them. There was a legend on Neverland of a boy who could fly and slay pirates. Realize that it had been so long for the boys. Peter had forgotten about them, and they had forgotten about Peter. Regardless of when or how long they had been on the island, a whole eternity could seemingly pass on Neverland even if it were only mere days or perhaps a generation in the real world. While he was away looking for Allison, Peter had faded into the mythology of the island, mostly spread through stories that the natives told. In this time, the lost boys were led by a new captain. As Peter remained balanced in the air, the new captain revealed himself.

"Come down, bird, and fight fairly!" The new captain cried; he was armed with a spear that he stole long ago from a native.

Slowly, Peter lowered himself to the ground and was lunged at by two others who were fiercely loyal to the new captain, but Peter killed them quickly—his eyes never leaving the new captain's. Again, Peter outstretched his arms as if to tell the new captain that his days were numbered. Allison watched from the distance, her heart sinking, all she could see were flashbacks of Billy. Out of sheer panic, she climbed down the tree and took off into the woods in such an impressive sprint that everything around her became one green blur.

She just wanted to get away and be safe, but the poor girl would have a troublesome time doing this because closing in from the sides were two lost boys clothed in wolf-skin.

These were two of the fastest of all the lost boys and every bit of their skill could match that of what cloaked them. Scraping past trees and bursting through low bushes, all of which seemed to purposely sabotage her escape, made it easy for one of the two to cut in front of her, causing a collision of still damp skin against fur. One more attempt was made to run away, but the second lost boy stood so firmly that she was knocked to the ground with a terrible crack.

Looking up into the faces of her hunters, she thought for sure that she saw fangs—they were feral enough. These boys, if that's really what they were, were no older than her. One started to circle her while the other stood directly over her and raised his spear to execute the fatal blow. It's difficult to describe accurately how someone feels or what someone thinks just moments before death, but for Allison, there was a sudden return to the theory that she was only in a dream. It didn't make her heart steady in the slightest, but there was a small gleam of hope that gave her strength to brace herself for any pain that might find her before waking in the real world. So, she closed her eyes and turned her head, but the blow never fell. A third lost boy leaped into the situation yelling at the other two to stop.

"That's a girl, you fool!" the new one snapped, knocking the spear aside and standing in the way; "Cowards strike girls." His voice was different, older than what she ever heard on the mainland, unless she were watching a time period movie.

"Captain did not hold your sentiment when we caught them in the spring," the spear holder said hotly.

"Them? There are two?" Her savior asked.

"Yes, her and a boy," said the other lost boy.

The spear holder stepped boldly into the new lost boy's space. "If killing a girl is so cowardly, maybe *you* should do it. One cowardly kill is better than none at all."

Allison's protector looked down at her, she couldn't quite tell if he was maybe weighing the pros and cons of what her hunters proposed. There was a moment of silence between them all. Allison remained frozen and waiting for the dream to end. She should have known that it was too good to last. All dreams eventually turn into nightmares. It was just a matter of time. Just when her mind began fantasizing about people that might be waiting for her back in that small town, even if it were around a hospital bed or grave, a fourth voice rang out from behind her.

"Your new captain might thin every one of you out if you touch her!"

"Peter!" Allison cried.

He stood in all his glory as true captain of Neverland, stern and dangerous.

"Pan!" Others shouted in remorseful remembrance.

It was a name that made two of the lost boys salute and sent the spear holder to his knees. Peter was covered in blood, flanked by eight lost boys. Most of them were older, perhaps rule breakers, but one was still very small. No one dared to ask where the other four were or where the former captain was. One thing was universally understood without a single word being passed among them, it was too plain on everyone's faces, no one would be going to the spring anytime soon.

***

For the rest of the day, Allison saw very little of Peter. Wherever Peter was, it is certain that he is surrounded by six of the lost boys, divvying up new roles and jobs for each of them. Chase and Dash would remain the top hunters. These were the boys dressed in wolfskins. Then there was Tom who wore a lion's skin. The three others were always dressed as bears and their names are as follows: Finn, Ned, and Joss. The two that were missing were Will and Benjamin who were watching Allison. She was left alone in a camp, which had been made by the lost boys during Peter's disappearance from Neverland. Will was very young. He clung to Benjamin's leg out of fear because he had forgotten what a girl was, so in his view, she was some kind of fairytale creature that was either good or bad and he was waiting to see which it would be. Benjamin was the second oldest of the lost boys and the kindest. He had the most memories of what the real world is, but rarely would he speak of it mostly because, up until now, there was no one who would care to listen. It was already challenging enough to fit in with the others, but speaking of a past none of them would remember—it's best to remain flowing together in one direction on this island.

Allison was seated by the fire, which was centered in the camp. With Peter away from her, thoughts came back. Flashes of her world, blurry faces, and fears were crashing against her mind. Crickets and night sounds were congregating around areas beyond the reach of the fire's wavering glow. It was increasingly important to her that her eyes remained fixed on the flames. If her sight wandered into anyplace untouched by the glow, she would see awful shadows and strange things that would move and grow if she focused on them. But it was harder said than done to keep her sight on something other than the darkness.

"Poor Alice," Benjamin appeared at her side.

"I prefer Allison." She said it coldly at first before she identified Benjamin as being the same voice of reason that prolonged her life long enough for Peter to find them. The realization gave her a sorry look.

Benjamin nodded in response to her preference. He sat quietly for a little while and watched his fingers fiddle with each other. The smile on his face made Allison feel at peace that he was friendly, but she still was cautious. She subtly scanned the camp to see if Peter was anywhere close. She really wasn't sure about him yet; however, she opted that it might be important to keep her former rescuer peaceful.

"What do they call you?" she asked, to look more receptive of his apparent hospitality.

"Benjamin."

She furrowed her brows. "Nice."

Benjamin nodded and kept smiling. Allison felt confused about what to say next. There was nothing but the fire crackling for a few short minutes. Eventually, it became uncomfortable enough that she looked into the flames and positioned herself to hopefully give off the time-to-leave-me-alone vibe, but Benjamin took her awkwardness as an opportunity to get to know her. It had been so long since he could speak to someone who had more than hunting or adventures on the mind, someone still fresh from the mainland.

"I hope we didn't scare you too much today," Benjamin said gently. It did the trick.

"I have only been that scared a few times in my life before. The only thing keeping me from losing it is knowing that this is all just some crazy realistic state of unconsciousness." Benjamin looked at her intently and mirrored the way she was sitting.

He half smiled. "You think you're dreaming?"

She shrugged and fell silent again, so Benjamin shared more about his experience.

"I understand." He leaned forward and looked into the fire. "There were at least thirty other boys on the island when I arrived, but as you can see, numbers rise and fall." Benjamin glanced at her to judge her reaction.

"You mean you all just keep killing each other?" she said, unsettled.

"It bothers you?"

"Doesn't it you?"

"Yes." Benjamin frowned. "You're Peter's though. As long as you're with him, you'll be safe enough."

Allison paused and pursed her lips. He was quiet, too, but he started to watch her, sensing that something was on her mind.

"What are you thinking?" he said.

Her eyes flickered to his and she laughed a little. "I'm thinking that you talk funny." Her response caught him off guard, causing him to chuckle.

"I mean, where are you from?" she said, trying to rephrase her question to sound less rude.

"I am from somewhere... old." He eyed her again.

"Okay," she said, her tone encouraging him to continue.

Once his thoughts had been properly arranged, he scooted a bit closer to Allison. "It was the Golden Age of Piracy in your world," he said.

Her brows lifted. "Mid-18th century?"

"Right as a fair wind, Lass." Benjamin grinned brightly.

That piqued Allison's curiosity, but when a fiery glare from across the camp made Benjamin shoot up from his position by her, the flighty lost boy bid Allison pleasant dreams before disappearing inside a tent. Peter's approach was calm and urgently curious. He took Benjamin's place and grinned falsely.

"If that one was bothering you, Allison," Peter gestured to the tent; "I'll ensure he doesn't again."

"He wasn't." Allison reassured him as she shifted her weight.

Nervousness ceased Peter's stomach. He stood up abruptly and offered his hand to Allison. It was past that usual time when he would take her back to the treehouse, like it or not.

"I kinda want to stay," she said. "I want to find Benjamin."

Peter's eyes became darker. In the fire's glow, he stood there taking deep controlled breaths.

"It's better that you come with me," he said.

"Peter, I don't want to right now." She shot him a look.

Peter's head filtered through a hundred ways he could get what he wanted. The most prominent solution was to do what he had always done, but the look on her face was more stubborn now than times before. He knew that forcing her would upset her. He didn't want to get *that* aggressive, not if he could help it. So, he nodded and found an excuse to leave her alone, just shortly, before he would return and try again. She got what she wanted but somehow, she felt bothered. Standing up and forgetting about the shadows and shapes she thought she saw beyond the fire's safety border, she left camp and walked into the dense jungle. She paused when she felt she was comfortably far enough away.

"You should not wander alone," Benjamin said, his tone measured.

Brushing her fingers over some large leaves, she glanced over her shoulder. "I wasn't planning on going far."

His eyes scanned her eyes, and his voice was deliberately quieter. "That does not matter. This place… it has a way of changing people without them even knowing.”

Allison titled her head, curious, sensing that there was more to what he said. “You mean the island?”

He looked straight at her though it was dark. “I mean him,” he said, then paused. “He is charming, aye? Easy to have fun with, easy to trust.” Benjamin’s jaw tightened almost unnoticeably. “But easy might not always be safe.”

She squinted, surprised by his sudden tone. “Like, you think he’s dangerous?”

He exhaled and briefly looked away before he returned his eyes to her own. “I think you should be careful,” he said, his voice lowering. “Not everyone who makes you feel something like this is leading you somewhere good.”

A sudden breeze stirred the trees and threaded through her hair, causing her to hug herself. She realized how close he had managed to get to her. Aside from the wind, the space between them felt still but weighted.

She took a step backward, hesitant, watching him. "You don't know anything about how I'm feeling."

Benjamin let a small, humorless chuckle out, his gaze darkened with unreadability. "Maybe not." He stepped back, pulling himself from the conversation before it went too far. He looked almost regretful. "Just… don't get lost, alright?"

Before she could say anything else, he walked away back toward camp, leaving her questioning, standing somewhere in the midst of the distant safety of camp and the shadows of the island. Lost in thought, she slowly made her way back to camp. Peter saw her return. He was leaning against a tree, his brows knit, and his arms crossed. Pushing himself off the tree, he approached her.

"I don't like you leaving," Peter said, his voice nearly a violent whisper.

Allison ignored his tone. She wanted an answer to something.

"Would you hurt me?"

Peter blinked. He hadn't expected that.

She looked at him, enunciating her words again. "Would you hurt me?"

"Never," he said firmly but softly, carefully.

"You said that one night, when we first met, that I wouldn't be like the others. What did you mean?" she said.

He was hesitant, uncertain if even now was the best time to share. What if she didn't understand?

He swallowed. "I meant that I would save you."

Allison stepped closer to him, her eyes penetrating his. "From what?"

Peter's voice became lower with rash hatred. "Your world… is cruel and unfair. It demands too much, ruthlessly controlling everything until it's all used up and there's nothing left to do than make everything old and dead."

"My world's hard but it's not like people don't die here, too."

Peter's expression turned unbelieving. "People who die here deserve it! That makes a big difference between your world and Neverland."

"How do you know when someone deserves death?" she asked.

This question stumped Peter not because he didn't know but because he did, he just didn't want to explain it to Allison. So, instead of answering, he let his shoulders slump. The last thing he wanted to get into right now was his mutiny against the way things are. He lost himself in thought for a moment, remembering the girls before Allison and how each of them betrayed him, simply because they couldn't free themselves from the fundamentals.

Allison noticed his jaw tense, so she took another step and gently squeezed his arm, bringing him back to the present and letting him know that everything was fine—that she would let it go. Peter smiled, but it left just as quickly, clearly forced for her sake. When he offered his other hand to her, she took it without resistance and allowed him to escort her back to the treehouse. She saw no good in forcing explanation if it upset him. She could sense it wouldn't be smart.

They lit candles to expel some of the night gloom and once there was sufficient light, they slipped into bed, beneath the furs. For the first time on the island, sleep was a difficult space to reach. She watched the ceiling or turned her head to gaze into the neighboring treetops, catching sight of a fairy once in a while. For Peter's sake, it was good that sleep waited to visit Allison. Her mind replayed how swiftly and heartlessly Peter had killed some of the lost boys. Only when she heard Peter crying in his sleep did those thoughts melt away—like snow in March. In this moment, he looked perfectly harmless. This innocence bewitched her to hold him tightly to herself until his sobbing turned to soft breaths. It's always so easy to pity a boy in tears.

Chapter Eleven

In time, the fleeting images and fear that Peter was dangerous in some way turned back into a view of intrigue. To Allison, he was still a protector and the lost boys, at least outwardly, confessed him as being their captain and would loyally do what was commanded of them. Many of the lost boys saw him as a leader and would follow orders because they felt good about falling into rank, but for a few others, fear was a leading cause for their obedience. Dash hadn't the stomach to do the killing and skinning that the others could. It wasn't a pleasant thing to him; he hated the way that the animals would squirm. Will was just a child who couldn't keep up with the rest. In fact, Allison noticed it was a daily struggle for him to even get food without her help. It usually took a stern look at the others to let Will get what he wanted. And Benjamin, he was never the type to run completely wild. He would do what was necessary to fit it, but it was clear to anyone paying attention that his heart was somewhere else.

It's not at all surprising that Allison would catch herself being more drawn to this trio. She pitied Dash and Will but had intense curiosity for Benjamin. Some days she would purposely do some form of chore that would place her in his proximity. She would then attempt to talk, but Peter always managed to show up, and at that point, Benjamin would refuse to even look at her. In fact, they were mostly distant. At first, she passed it off as them simply being shy about female presence, but the distance would only grow more exaggerated when Peter was around them. It was something that became grimly final when one evening, she noticed that Will scurried to his tent without even attempting to get food once Peter arrived at the table. Quickly making a plate amongst the noise, Allison escaped from the table and followed Will who was curled up in the corner of the tent with his arms wrapped securely around his thin knees.

"Aren't you hungry?" Allison spoke as softly as possible, like coaxing an abused puppy to take something out of her hand. When he looked up at her, there was unease but no fear. "You have to eat so you can be strong someday," she encouraged.

"Strong as they are?" the little boy said, his eyes showing a slight gleam.

"Oh, stronger!"

Standing up, he rushed to her side, and she settled to the ground and held the plate while he ate. When he was a little over half finished, she asked him what he thought about Peter.

"A god who kills us when we misbehave." The little boy shuddered and almost lost his appetite.

"Where did you hear that?" Allison kept her voice gentle, wanting to hear more about what the boy thought, but he was too busy working on eating.

When the little boy finished his plate, and though still shy of her, he lay on her lap while she hummed to him, the way a mother would. Now that he was in her arms, she felt outraged about how thin the boy actually was, but his head was on her chest, so she took some deep breaths so that her heart would not wake him. She sat lost in thought, trying to imagine how a conversation with Peter would go if she were to tell him to show the boys some comfort. Perhaps it was a good thing that Peter had finally noticed Allison's absence from him and decided to look for her whereabouts.

He was standing at the mouth of the tent, watching Allison rock the child, a sight that was familiar to him because it was precisely what those like Wendy and Jane had done to the smallest of the lost boys so many moons ago. Finally, Allison felt his staring and looked up to meet his surprisingly calm face. She hated to risk upsetting him, but it was necessary. With another deep breath, she seized a rather authoritative tone.

"Peter, something needs to change." She braced herself for a potential outburst, but he stood still and shrugged.

"Like what," he said.

Her eyes widened out of quiet exasperation, cradling the boy a little tighter when he stirred. "He was going to go hungry rather than sit and eat with you around!"
After a moment of silence and no movement from Peter, Allison looked more sternly at Peter, her voice getting more annoyed.

"Somehow, you see me as worth 'saving' from something. I know you dislike my world—there's truth in what you say about it,

I see it too. But Peter..." she looked down at Will, "the cruelty of this world will be no different if something isn't done."

Peter narrowed his eyes. "There's food, a secure camp."

"But no rights."

Now Peter thought he understood. Of course, all girls want to be mothers, and he never properly introduced her according to her role. All at once, the look on her face alarmed him so he rushed to her and kneeled beside her—carefully.

"Allison, you are to be with me always. It'll be like I'm their father, and you're their mother."

She was moved by the genuineness of his voice. It was a hopeful thing for her, the way he wanted to do better, but she wanted to make something a little clearer. She explained that being strict was fine—but there had to be balance. This led her to further open up about being troubled by the death of the former captain and lost boys. She feared the brutality of it, but Peter never really thought about the death of the boys as something frightening.

The only thoughts that did grieve him were flashes of things that happened that didn't really happen. It was his imagination cycling through all the bad things that would have happened if he hadn't killed. These visions came from his nightmares, hazy but violent and lonely. The fear in his heart grew overwhelming. Neverland could not become a dangerous place to her because, if she viewed it to be, then he would risk her demanding to leave. A vision of her begging to go back caused a little shudder to pass through him. He would never allow her to leave. The idea of forcing her disgusted him. He would never have pleasure in doing that to her, he'd rather it be willing.

"You know, Allison," Peter swallowed. "Neverland was once a place of pirates, but I fought them all. The lost boys who betrayed me would have become just as wicked. Now that they are slain, the island is safe for us all."

So, Peter—being charming and understanding his new role well enough—took Will from her lap and tucked him into his bed. Then he turned to Allison.

"I want to show you what has been saved," he said, giving a little crooked grin.

Reaching his hand out to hers, he peered into her eyes, his chin dipping down just far enough to accentuate his inviting eyes and just how beautifully framed with dark lashes they were. His plan was to fly her over the most beautiful parts of Neverland to give her a little preview of what he had planned for the next day. He blinked and his crooked grin grew more urgent when she hesitated to take his hand, but once she accepted it, he walked her into the woods. To her surprise, he didn't pay any attention when the sky darkened. By this time, they'd already be tucked in the treehouse, but this time it was different. The night air was crisp, and the farther Peter led her, she swore she could hear water crashing and smell the salt. She worried a bit, afraid. When Peter gave her hand a squeeze, she flinched, wondering if she had said any concerns out loud. Before long, Allison could look past Peter's shoulder and indeed see an opening—or more specifically, an end. The woods opened up to a cliff. Pushing past the large island leaves, Peter led Allison to the edge of the cliff, overlooking the shores and the glistening ocean below them. Not once did Peter let her hand go, even when her breath caught as he walked closer to the drop off. She had stopped cold, resisting. A look of pain replaced his crooked grin.

"Come on," he said. Peter gave her a gentle tug, testing her response.

Allison eyed him warily. "You want me to just… trust you? We're in the middle of me basically telling you off and you take me to a cliff."

Peter grinned, a hint of mischief dancing in his eyes. "I want you to trust gravity—or rather, my thorough disregard for it."

Allison crossed her arms. "That's not at all comforting."

Peter laughed, taking a closer step towards her since she refused to budge.

"Come on. It's not like this is your first time. Haven't you missed being close to me above the ocean. Here's your chance." Peter tilted his head with a smirk across his lips and a raised brow, but his voice was soft. "Unless you're afraid?"

"I'm not scared." Allison lifted her chin.

Peter's grin widened. "Then prove it."

Before she could change her mind or overthink her situation, Peter swept her up like she weighed nothing, one arm under her knees and the other arm securely around her waist. At once, the ground began to disappear beneath them, and the wind rushed around them, whipping her hair in front of her eyes as if each little strand knew it was too soon for her to see how high they had gone in so short of time. She still clutched to him, after so many flights before, she was still fearful. Peter's heart dropped a little, but he had an idea.

"Let me show you something." His breath was warm against her ear compared to the wind, making her skin turn to goosebumps.

He soared higher, his hold on her sure and strong. The island rolled beneath them, reminding her of so many childhood dreams she had forgotten until now. The ocean shimmered even in the darkness and the waves were curling in lovely patterns, crashing to the shore like silver on gold. Dipping through clouds, the cool mist contradicting Peter's warmth, making it easier and easier for Allison to press against him.

"You can open your eyes, you know," Peter said, he teased with his tone but was still so careful to be warm.

"I know, I am." She rapidly blinked, amazed at how many sensations flight could arouse. "I am." She looked at Peter, sensing his eyes on her. "This is—"

He watched her. "Complete… freedom."

The island expanded below them, glowing silver from the moonlight, boundless and wild from the dense forests that covered the island. Allison beheld it in awe.

"It's beautiful…" she said.

"You're seeing it now? What I've been trying to show you, trying to make you understand."

Feeling his heartbeat quicken, she turned to him, realizing he wasn't just talking about the island—he was talking about everything, the adventure, the freedom and maybe…them.

Peter's voice was barely above a whisper. He leaned closer like they weren't the only two people flying around like birds. "Stay."

That word lingered between them, only met with silence, as weightless but heavy enough to make her feel pulled down from the moment of bliss. She met his gaze, noticing that they were descending, perhaps he felt the same heaviness.

"I'm feeling tired now," she said, looking down at the fabric of her blouse, hoping that he wouldn't push the matter any further.

She dared another glance. This time, he looked distant—lost. The moment stretched between them even when they reached the ground in the midst of the woods. She recognized it as not far from the treehouse. Not yet putting her down, he gazed into her eyes, which were carrying still unspoken things. For the first time, she started to wonder what exactly she should be afraid of.

When they made it back to the treehouse, he was more than anxious to go to bed so that he could keep his arms securely around her and pretend she'd never try to slip away. He did hold her all night and imagined how lovely she would be swimming with mermaids, or all covered with wishes on Dandelion Hill. Above all, he was determined to make Neverland the only home she could ever remember.

Chapter Twelve

The next day unfolded almost exactly according to Peter's plan—*almost*. He kept her so busy. He showed her Mermaid Lagoon, which was quite fun, though Peter was careful not to turn his back to Allison while a mermaid was too close, fearing that she might be drowned by one. Mermaids, like fairies, could be devious, jealous things. There was an array of other sights as well, like Crystal Falls and the mouth of Echoe Woods—a dark forest, not really woods, full of voices and forces—a place where none were allowed to go, by Peter's order. When she asked about the "woods," Peter would brush the question off and insisted that there were better places on the island. So, he took her hiking to Dandelion Hill.

As the name would suggest, it was a large hill, more of a meadow, that was covered in dandelions—very unlike those on the mainland. Some dandelions were only ankle high, but most grew so tall that just brushing past them turned the ends of Allison's hair white. The meadow was warmer than the wooded parts of the island, when the sun shone directly. Honeybees buzzed lazily, drifting from a little yellow flower to another. The wild grass turned white in the breeze and glistened in the sunshine. Allison followed Peter further into the meadow until Peter stopped, stretched, and crossed his arms, smiling brightly—his hair a shade lighter in the golden glow. He spent a moment just standing still and looking around at the meadow, at the woods bordering the other side of the meadow. He took a deep breath and closed his eyes.

"What are you thinking of?" she said, taking a step closer to him.

Peter nudged her hand with his own and grinned. "You know if you listen, Allison, you can hear all the wishes of youth from all over the mainland," he said.

To prove it, he moved behind her and covered her eyes with both of his hands. Then, he leaned near her ear. "You can hear them, if we're completely quiet."

She took a deep breath and held still, trying to not even let her feet make the grass squeak. She tried to focus on the silence, imagining what these voices must sound like, but Peter's breath by her ear continually scattered her thoughts. She almost gave up until many soft whispers rose around them, quiet and layered, like prayers.

"Peter, I hear them!" she breathed. She looked at him, delighted, but he scowled, alarmed. "What, really? I was joking!"

Allison blinked, her brows narrowing as she tried to think of a response, but Peter's expression broke and he laughed out loud.

"You—" She removed his hands from her eyes and swatting his arm with the back of her hand in one swift motion.

Peter kept laughing while she stood there, her blush deepening.

"Oh, whatever!" she said, crossing her arms.

She tried to look stern, like his cliché joke wasn't at all funny. But it humored him further that that was her response, so she hit him again. Unbothered, Peter regained control of his laughter and fell back into the grass, sending a cloud of wishes into the sky. He lay there on his back with his hands folded behind his head, his eyes beautifully half-lidded—content.

"You know, I like coming here as often as I can."

Allison glanced down at him, her hair falling more in front of her face. She was half amused, half in awe.

"Yeah?"

Peter grinned and lifted his chin to glance back at her before closing his eyes. "Mm-hmm."

"Why?" she asked.

She knew why, she just wanted to make him talk. The question caused his brow to lift, and he hummed to himself. Allison knelt down beside him, giving him a little nudge when he still didn't answer. He chuckled and opened his eyes to stare at her, eyes still half-lidded.

"Everything here's always so warm, the air smells like these," He paused, plucking a little yellow flower and sitting up just enough to tuck it into her hair, "and now you're sitting right beside me."

Then he lay back down, and she smiled. Sunshine lit his face up, decorating his hair in highlights.

"Do you have wishes?" she asked.

Peter smiled at her and sat up completely. Scooting a bit closer so that his sweet breath tinkled her nose and pink cheeks, he raised a brow and got a crooked grin across his lips. She watched his eyes flicker between her eyes and her lips. It gave her such a funny feeling, a feeling so desirable that she allowed him to close more space between them.

"It's unfair," Peter said.

Allison blinked, her blush turning deeper. "Unfair?"

He gave her a solemn nod. "Mmm."

"Why?"

"Because there's only one thing missing."

Allison tilted her head, curious. "Like what?"

"Like something I've wanted since the first time I saw you, something maybe—" a beautiful smirk overthrew his grin "—like a kiss."

Her gaze dropped in a hurry, tugging at her hair, she looked past her toes to the little white butterflies dancing ahead. "You're not very subtle," she said, swallowing.

Peter untangled her fingers from her hair and held her hands lightly between his hands. "Oh? I thought I was being romantic." He brushed his thumb over her knuckles. "I'd like to be more direct..."

A sweet breeze stirred the tall dandelions, sending a cloud of white into their space and into their hair like January snow. Neither of them moved for a moment, her fingers hesitated but cautiously curled. He leaned closer, his eyes studying hers. Another moment later and his hand was behind her neck, his head titling and closing more space between them until only their upper lips teasingly touched. So close to a kiss. But Allison sighed and pulled away as soon as Peter felt confident enough to close his lovely eyes. When his lips failed to feel hers and his eyes reopened, there were frustration building in his eyes.

"What must I do to have you?" Peter cried, pounding the ground with his fist.

"It's nothing that you can really do," she answered, terribly embarrassed. "It's just that, well, I want to really make sure that I'm in love with the next guy I kiss."

He shot her a look, surprised that she'd actually response to his rhetorical statement. "Have you kissed before?" he said, trying to hide his hatred of whoever kissed her first.

He could see that her hidden kiss was still secured in the corner of her mouth, so he was, although upset, filled with some level of pride knowing that this special kiss was his alone to have. She took one steady breath; he met her eyes again when she tried to answer his question.

"Well, yeah." She hesitated for the right words. "I feel like I've already lost parts of myself that I'll never get back. The next time will be different."

Peter shook his head in disbelief. "But it's already different," he insisted. "You are mine and this is our home forever and ever." Peter used his body to ease the girl to lay flat on her back so that he was positioned over her. "Allison..."

She looked at him with aching tenderness. Nothing could describe how tempting it truly was. He was the loveliest, and with the way the wind blew through the dandelions and released more nearly inaudible whispers, it felt nearly criminal to resist him. All the wishes around them couldn't equal the amount of desire in her. With heaviness in her heart, her head leaned to the left and she blinked to cope.

Peter shuddered and breathed quick breaths. He had half a mind to take the kiss by force, but something deeper inside warned him that she would surely loath him for it. The best thing for both of them would be distance, which is precisely what Peter would do. Without so much as a goodbye, he stood up and stormed off. This could be seen as cold and unreasonable to leave her so abruptly, but don't judge too much. Instead of flying, he walked so that she could easily follow his footprints and find her way back to the treehouse. This angry distancing was a habit that kept them safe from so many things, but Peter was most concerned about how Allison viewed him. In her eyes, he wanted to be gentle and heroic, the perfect choice to play house with.

Chapter Thirteen

"Peter, wait!" she had called after him, her mind flipping between steadfastness and regret.

She remained on Dandelion Hill for a while, and when she finally left and ventured back into the trees to follow him, a part of her felt awful for hurting him. It's exactly the kind of conflict she wanted to avoid. It shocked her how incapable a boy is of just being in a girl's presence without expecting some form of romantic activity. It wasn't that she didn't desire romance, that wasn't the case; she dreamed of it often. But it was the responsibility and the drama that it brings that made her wary. Even the responsibility factor is complicated. She wanted to be the type who could be there for a love interest anytime of the day or night and be the kind of girl that a boy dreams about, but not at the expense of her own heart's readiness. In a strange and indescribable way, she loved Peter. He owned a piece of her heart even before she knew or remembered him; he was the déjà vu that can be experienced at random, someone who was always a part of her life and probably always will be.

In Neverland, this feeling only grows more intense because time is bolder and longer and there was a separation here that the mainland could only barely understand. Impulse and passion rule over all. Logic here can be used in games of make-believe, but in a flash, impulse and passion can crush it. Neverland, thus, becomes a darker and more dangerous place for those who have balance of each. This isn't to imply that Allison is balanced, and that Neverland is particularly dangerous to her. On the contrary, the logical few who find themselves in Neverland may navigate and usually find a way to escape, but the dreamers—they have a harder time seeing past the beauties. In essence, those with logic can see the darkness and danger of the place whereas the dreamer dismisses it until it's much too late.

At about this time, Allison was in front of the mouth of Echoe Woods. She beheld the depth of the place, almost as if she knew that there was a reason to stay for a while and there was. It started out as small as a firefly: a blue light fluttered into existence, unfolding until it grew into a blaze that hovered in midair. It was so lovely that she couldn't help staring in wonder. The more intent her stare became, she could see a shadow in the blue blaze, and it seemed to stare back at her and with one gracefully outstretched hand, it reached to her and beckoned. She obeyed it. That's another thing about dreamers; they are carelessly curious. So, leaving Peter's path, Allison followed the blue shadow as it lured her further by disappearing then reappearing in the new direction that it wanted her to take.

The light of the shadow was so brilliant that she failed to see just how tragically dark the forest was. It never crossed her mind how long she had been walking or how far from the path she had strayed. She looked down for only a moment to keep from tripping over a fallen branch and when she looked up again, the blue shadow vanished, causing her to come to a halt. As if awakened from a dream, she looked around her and saw the darkness. There was no way to find Peter's path again. She couldn't remember how many rights or lefts she had taken, and finding footprints was equally impossible. At once tears pooled in her eyes. Hugging herself, she hung her head and began to shuffle forward, her steps slow and cautious for fear of falling.

It was a good thing that she walked this way because if she hadn't then she wouldn't have accidentally kicked that pill bottle that she had pocketed before she left home. She recognized the sound and immediately dropped to her knees to search for it. When she located it, she continued to search for the phone, which she found eventually. Clutching the items, her heart felt like it had sunk to a place far out of her reach and there was just hollowness. Something about the darkness of the woods made her want to open the little bottle, so she tried, but it didn't work. The more she tried, the more frustration built inside her. With the coldness of evening settling into the island air, she wondered again if she was actually dead—and if she had been lied to about what Hell really was. Trying to open the bottle again, Allison burst into tears, almost ready to pick herself off the ground to just wander. Sobbing, she stood up and wiped her face. The air was so gloomy, all she could do was feel heavy. She stumbled forward, plagued by intrusive thoughts when a pair of hands spun her around and she was yanked back to the living by Peter's tightening grip and furious expression. Dash and Benjamin were standing a short distance away, each with a torch in hand. Benjamin's eyes stared extra hard but not from inconvenience like Dash's expression—it was from concern instead, almost fear. Their earlier conversation—Benjamin's warning about the island, about Peter—rushed back into her memory. Peter's jaw was so tensed that his cheeks were sunken, and his eyes sliced into hers.

Peter's breathing was deep and deliberate, his presence more brooding than she had ever seen.

"I was waiting for you," he said.

Allison swallowed, opening her mouth to offer some form of excuse but nothing would come. Her eyes flickered to Benjamin's who nodded subtly. She thought a little harder, unknowingly fingering the bottle. The small objects inside of it rattling as the bottle turned in her fingers. Peter's ears caught the noises.

Grabbing the bottle viciously, he sneered at her. "What is this thing?" he spat.

"You know what it is," Allison murmured, rubbing her fingers from the knuckles down.

It suddenly dawned on her that maybe he was the one who took it away from her, perhaps while she was sleeping. The accusation was in her eyes, causing Peter's upper lip to lift from anger. He saw the redness in her eyes and deathly air was still clinging to her like a wet dress. An internal panic squeezed his insides and flashes of her cemetery stone squeezed extra hard.

"It's not real," he said, taking the bottle.

He held the item in his hands, and it turned to dust. Then, leaning close to Allison and gripping her shoulder again, he stared at her and she couldn't tell if he was threatening her or purely offering advice.

"The secret to youth is forgetting," he said.

Allison's silence broke, her voice barely above a whisper. "I try, Peter."

Peter's face turned unreadable. He took her by the wrist and started walking in Dash and Bejamin's direction, pulling Allison with him. As they passed Benjamin, he gave her a sorry look before he and Dash followed behind with their torches held high. He could have flown the two of them out of the forest, but he wanted Allison to struggle keeping up with him as he dragged her back to the main path. Finally making it back to the treehouse, Peter stood on the balcony and watched her. He had the kind of angry eyes that made her slouch and carefully slip by him in fear that he might hit at any moment. The whole time, he never said a word. He only watched her as she dressed for bed and coaxed herself to sleep. He hoped that she was ashamed enough and tired enough to remain sleeping. He needed time to think of a new plan.

They all leave, he thought grimly. *But this time will be different.*

Chapter Fourteen

Allison woke up in the treehouse bedroom, relaxed at first but quickly anxious upon remembering the previous day. With the birds chirping and cooing or drumming and the frogs trilling, the island seemed happy enough. It was her deepest hope that Peter would be in an equally good mood. Hurting him was the last thing she wanted to do. She felt worse about what had happened. Her time on the island might have been what some adventurers would call perfect. The island was a magical place, with sights and feelings unlike anything on the mainland. And Peter… there was always something about him, sweet and suffocating at the same time. But she couldn't help being reminded of home some of the time. Entering Echoe Woods had brought back such a strange grief that it was hard for her to shake. It was the blue shadow that had some strange effect on her and her actions. These were the topics that she wanted to discuss with Peter. She ached to tell him how terribly sorry she was.

Slipping from under the furs and walking to the balcony, she leaned against it to watch some of the lost boys playing battle games. She imagined them as truly being her sons. Fluttering of wings brushed past her ears and she witnessed two lovestruck fairies—one lovely girl dressed in tulip petals and the boy dressed in pinecone armor—zipping by and landing in the treetops. Maybe Peter was right. Maybe she should kiss him. This was a happy place, not perfect, but it was happy. And Peter, he was far from perfect, but he was everything she wanted when she thought about it. She wanted so badly to tell him her decision, to wrap her arms around his neck and give him the kiss. So, she dressed and stepped out onto the balcony, somewhat expecting that Peter would drop in. But he didn't. She looked around but if he was there, he was out of her sight, which worried her. It was unlike him to leave her alone. A feeling of abandonment ghosted her heart.

She climbed carefully down from the treehouse and scanned the bordering woods as soon as her feet were securely grounded. Benjamin was the first to fall into her sight. He was sitting on a cut tree stump like he had been waiting for her. She inhaled, still feeling embarrassed for having been lured into those woods and lost. She held her head low as she approached him.

"Where's Peter? I need to talk to him about what happened yesterday," Allison said, her eyes searching for some sign of his presence like flashes of movement behind the trees or something.

"Peter has been gone for a whole day," Benjamin answered.

She shot him a confused little look, which caused Benjamin to offer an explanation. "You slept a long time." He told her.

"Impossible!"

Benjamin shrugged, watching her face. "He thought it best to let you rest."

Allison sighed, sensing there was more to his words. "I wasn't that tired..."

She eyed Benjamin for any sign that maybe he would say something to make things make sense, but when he glanced down at his feet, she knew it would be pointless to hope. Brushing that topic aside, she did feel put off that Peter would leave without telling her, but she would make allowance since she reasoned to herself that she had been the difficult one lately.

"Well, when will he be back." Allison asked, taking a subtle breath to hide her annoyance.

"He said he'd signal when he returns."

Allison was beyond distraught to hear that, but this was the price to pay, that's what she thought. Though she knew that she deserved to feel this way, she couldn't help but show her disappointment by slumping her shoulders and looking rather glum in the face. It was a look that Benjamin hated to see on a girl, so he offered his arm to her.

"I bet you're starved. Let's get you something to eat." He smiled though she only gave him a half smile back.

It was quieter around them now because most of the lost boys had ducked into the woods to further their game, which was perfectly fine with Benjamin who had already had a gut full of them. Once he had Allison comfortably seated, he sat down beside her and watched her in silence while she got a few bites of fruit swallowed. Wiping the juice from the sides of her mouth, she smiled more full-heartedly at the birds that constantly flew overhead.

"You seem different today." Benjamin remarked.

"I think it's because I am different."

Benjamin raised both his brows, a clear-cut prompt that he wanted her to expand her comment. She smiled a little and returned her attention to another piece of fruit.

"Neverland is so beautiful," she said.

"You say it like you are trying to convince yourself," Benjamin said.

"It *is* beautiful. And it's everything I've ever wanted. It's certainly not boring. I mean, I've written about stuff like this, memorized scripts, watched it in the movies, and thought 'how great would that be.'" Allison glanced at Benjamin, realizing that he probably didn't understand some of the things she mentioned, like movies. She sighed. "In time, things will only get better here. I'm finally done being alone or feeling out of place like I did back home."

"You speak like you lived in a convent," Benjamin jested.

"Worse; a small town."

Benjamin grinned and shook his head. "I lived in a little fishing town with my father. Life was far beyond lonely. People, at least in my town, always had each other's back," He said, his face and tone trying to hide how strongly he felt about her insult.

Allison stopped herself from rolling her eyes. Benjamin placed his hand over hers and looked her very sternly in the eyes. Her eyes widened, looking back at him, deliberating about pulling her hand away.

"I am surprised that you feel that way after what happened to you in Echoe Woods," he said.

This time, she knew for sure that he meant more than what was said.

Allison shrugged. "So, I got lost. It happens."

Benjamin frowned. "That is not what I am referencing."

"Then just what are you referencing?" She huffed. "My gosh, if you have something to say just say it! Or are you just that afraid of Peter?"

Benjamin blinked, feeling like her outburst was uncalled for, but his face would never show it. It was more important to him for her to understand.

"You saw it, the blue shadow, that is what caused you to go off the path," he said.

"How did you—"

Benjamin inhaled and noted her alarm. "Because I, too, saw it."

"When?"

"When I first came here," he said, scanning the woods to make sure no one was listening. "Then… so many other times, more than I can count."

Allison blinked. "So, you know what it is? That's great!"

Benjamin shook his head.

Allison tilted her head, disappointed. "You don't know?"

"Can I trust you?"

"What?"

"Can I trust you?"

"Yes," she said, curious about what he would say.

Benjamin stood up and glanced around. There wasn't anyone nearby. For the first time since their first day meeting, Benjamin and Allison were as good as alone.

"Follow me," he said to her.

She gave him a questioning look, not quite knowing if it would be the smart thing to do but she couldn't help being intrigued. She stood with him and waited for him to take the lead. The island was bustling with bird calls and distant yelling from other lost boys. And with Peter away, she never felt freer in this place to finally do some exploring. At least this time, Benjamin was there. They slipped past the first several trees, but this only made Benjamin pick his pace up. Allison kept up the best she could, taking wider steps and groaning each time something caused her to semi-trip. It was still morning, so the Neverland plants were wet with dew, which made it all the harder for Allison because the big leaves would always hit her in the face if she failed to duck low enough. It annoyed her. Benjamin laughed when it happened for the twentieth time.

"Peter carries you so much, it looks like you forgot how to walk," he teased.

She rolled her eyes. "Funny guy."

Allison huffed, flinching when she came close to being hit by another leaf, but

Benjamin caught it in time and held it back. "Almost there. Be patient."

She lifted her brows. "Haven't I been?"

He shrugged.

"How much farther is 'almost there' anyway?"

Benjamin smiled. Holding back another branch of big leaves, he pointed to a large tree with a hollow place in it. He waited for her to step in front of him before he let go of the branch and jogged up ahead of her to the tree. He knelt down and brushed some loose ferns away from the inside base of a very large tree. His fingers started feeling around to find a groove. With a knowing smile, he lifted what appeared to be a lid that was as dark and weathered as the tree—almost seamlessly hiding it from anyone who's not purposefully looking.

Allison stepped closer, her eyes blinking with wonder. "A secret door?"

Benjamin's smile broadened, glad about her curiosity. "Aye! After you."

Allison hesitated a moment before she also crouched down to peer into the bottom of the hollowed-out trunk. It was a tunnel—passage sounds nicer—that descended into shadows. It smelled of aging wood and soil, curling up from the darkness. Bracing herself, looking briefly in Benjamin's eyes, she started to lower herself inside.

"Careful," he said. Benjamin's voice was soft, practically a whisper as his eyes darted between her footing and the surrounding woods behind him.

Allison's shoes scraped against the wooden trunk-tunnel as she descended. As soon as she was down all the way, she ducked to avoid a large root then turned in the direction where the tunnel opened into a hidden underground space. She smiled, noting how cozy and small it was. The air smelled like old parchment and ink and there were candles flickering in every corner, illuminating the uneven walls and the stacks of journals all piled on top of each other on a little homemade desk.

She glanced around again, nearly spinning in a full circle, taking in the scene—feeling perhaps a bit like a hobbit. "So, this is where you disappear to."

By now, Benjamin had squeezed down the tunnel and fixed his clothes, brushing away stray bark and dirt. He watched her in amusement but there was unspoken concern in his eyes. She trailed her fingers along the stack of journals. Her eyes were especially drawn to the careful script on the open title covers. Picking one up, she flipped through it. These books aren't just records of silly things; they're pieces of experiences—life—that no one else seems to remember on this island.

Her eyes darted up at Benjamin's, returning the look of wonder but also concern, her voice full of hesitation.

"Peter doesn't know about this place, does he?"

Benjamin shook his head, answering on an exhale. "No."

"Why?"

Benjamin took a breath and exhaled again, like he was trying to control being nervous. His eyes flickered to the journal in her hands, then back to her.

"He wouldn't understand." Taking the journal from her, he opened it to one of its worn pages before holding it back out to her. "He doesn't appreciate the things I do."

Allison took it and traced her fingers over the deliberate handwriting, like the words were some kind of lifeline. It looked like historical fiction complete with sketches, notes, and names.

"That was my father," he said, nodding to the sketch on the page.

"James. It's a good name." She looked around at the room again—all the books. "How long have you been…"

"Longer than I would like you to know." He laughed halfheartedly. "It might frighten you."

She scoffed. "Nah, I don't think so. But all this time, keeping it secret?"

Benjamin watched her brows knit like she was on the brink of understanding something.

His voice lowered, almost wary. "You've noticed, haven't you? The others… they can't express themselves like this."

Softly, that realization dawned on her. "I suspected they couldn't write."

Benjamin nodded, picking up another book and tightening his grip on it. "And neither can Peter. He can't, so nobody else can."

"That's terrible…" she said, lowering the journal until it was gingerly placed on the desk again.

Benjamin's lips pulled down into a distant expression.

"And so is the way of his kingdom."

Memories of Benjamin's previous warning about Peter and the island flashed back into her head. She always sensed a scrap between them.

"Why did you bring me here?" she said.

Benjamin blinked, caught a bit off guard by her straightforwardness. "Because you seem…conflicted."

"Conflicted?"

He nodded. "The woods—the blue shadow, not everyone sees it."

"What do you mean?"

Walking to another stack of books and pushing some of them aside, he thumbed through another journal and set it down open on the desk. He pointed to a sketch.

Allison shivered. "That's it. That's what I saw."

Benjamin fell silent, his mood shifting to something strange—hopeful.

Allison's brows scrunched as she touched his arm, cautiously prompting him to return to the moment. "What do you know?"

He blinked and looked down at her, stepping closer so that she needed to look up more sharply.

"I know that we are connected because we have regrets, things that are yet to be resolved. It is as though the island knows…" he said.

Allison tilted her head. "I'm not following."

"There must be someone missing you," Benjamin said.

Allison averted her eyes, her mouth opening slightly in a wordless way to say she didn't want to get into it. She almost shied away from him, but he caught her, holding her in place and looking more desperately into her eyes.

"No. Nobody," she said, flinching when she realized how defensive her tone was.

"No parents? No siblings?" he pressed.

Allison swallowed. "No one."

Benjamin watched her. She felt like he knew that she was lying, so she inhaled and shook her head repeatedly with that one breath held.

"I just… Nothing was ever the same again." She grimaced. "I envy those who were able to just forget," Allison confessed.

Benjamin frowned. "People are given memories for a reason."

"But there's no real need." She gestured to the whole of the place. "This is freedom! The woods the other day just reminded me of what Peter saved me from. There is nothing worse than that emptiness."

His voice was a whisper. "I regret my choice, Allison. I wish I had someone who could have warned me." He looked down at the still open book with the sketch of his father, he closed it one-handed. "Now, my regret will never be fixed, and each day is a conscious effort to not forget."

Allison's brows furrowed in pure inability to understand.

"But if you missed him so much, then why didn't you just leave the island?" she said.

Benjamin grinned but it wasn't a glad grin. "Peter is the only one who can fly." His voice picked up in tone, likely from very controlled anger. "The fairies are on his side, so no help ever comes from them."

"Why don't you ask him?"

It seemed the obvious thing to do in her mind.

"Allison, I don't think you see. Boys that come here are not allowed to leave." He started whispering again. "But you can. I was traveling before past a native camp, and I heard the wife of a brave telling their children that Peter allowed a group of lost boys to leave upon request of your ancestor—Wendy Darling."

Now it dawned on her fully. "You want me to ask Peter to let you leave?"

It took a moment of thought, mainly because she viewed the situation as exceedingly cowardly. Still, she nodded and told him that she would ask.

He grinned. "I know you'll be happy with your choice."

Her eyes flickered to him. "What? I'm not leaving," she corrected him.

"You must!" Benjamin said, nearly forgetting to whisper.

Allison stepped away from him. "Why would I?"

"Because you'll regret it for as long as Peter allows you to live." His face was serious, too serious.

Her eyes narrowed. She felt suddenly exposed. "What are you saying? Just spit it out," Allison said, stepping behind a support beam.

"Me, Dash, Will, none of us will leave this island alive without you with us. Right now, he cares about you as he once cared about your ancestors." He watched how she hid behind the beam as if she feared that he would take her from the island by force. It was a stance that caused a dull pain in his chest. He inhaled, prepared to convince her. "Peter is fickle, and I fear that someday he'll leave you here and disappear and when he comes back, he won't know you... He fears what he doesn't know."

Poor Allison didn't quite know how to take what he said. She had strong feelings for Peter even though he acted impossible sometimes. She deemed it insane to think that Peter would ever forget her. He obviously didn't forget her ancestors and he wanted her enough to have left Neverland for so long just to find her. There was an undeniable connection between them. He was protective, sure, but maybe for good reason. She knew how bitterly Peter would cry some nights—he wasn't a monster; monsters don't weep like that. Benjamin saw her blindness to Peter's coldness, so with a sigh he nodded in the direction of the tunnel. He waited for her by the tunnel. This time, he went first so that he could crack the wooden lid just enough to peer outside to check for signs of others. Then, he opened it completely and climbed out, giving her his hand as soon as he had his own footing secure.

"I want you see something." He told her.

***

He led her to the spring that she and Peter used when he first brought her to the island. She entered the clearing, happy at first—but then she froze, her face paling. There, precisely where Peter left them, were the bodies of the lost boys that fought against him upon their reunion. Benjamin walked further, he was willing to see them more up-close and he wanted Allison to do the same. Allison, however, was nearly sick at the thought, so she shook her head violently and stepped backward.

"I can't. I won't!" She cried, turned, and sprinted back into the woods.

Benjamin abandoned his plan to follow after her. Fearing that she would be sick if she got any closer, she stopped. She looked him in the face with total fear and disgust... refusal. She was still shaking her head.

Benjamin tried to keep his express soft. "It is not for any of us. Before it's too late, just think about it," he said, referring to the island—to Peter.

Her breath quickened.

"They had it coming," she rationalized. "Don't act like the mainland is any different, or was your town the exception?"

More could have been said and maybe Benjamin could have been able to persuade her, but Peter's crow fell on their ears and so did a mob of new voices. They returned to camp, the one beyond the treehouse, to see what Peter had brought from the mainland. Peter was rested on a tree branch bathing in the glory of how the new boys praised him. There had to be twenty, at least, but it was difficult to count because they were all running in various directions like a surprised flock of birds. Peter beamed with pride as he loudly declared them his new lost boys.

When he spotted Allison, he swooped down from the branch to greet her, a conqueror's joy lighting up his face. Throwing his arms around her, he smiled down at her. This was Peter's plan. Keep her busy. With so many new faces, some very young, she'd devote time tending to them, satisfying her role. Someday she'd forget about the mainland and love the life he'd provide.

Chapter Fifteen

Bringing more lost boys to the island did keep Allison busy, but she was increasingly unfond of the games that they would choose to play. The only solace she would find was with Will or sometimes Dash. For example, there was a day when she thought it was a good idea to go to the beach and collect things. It took very little convincing to get Will to join. Dash also went along with them because he thought it would be better than putting up with the new lost boys. It was rare for her to see Benjamin. He would spend days missing from camp and when he returned, he would be quiet and shielded. As for Peter, he never stopped trying to find ways to force proximity. Let's keep using that day at the beach as an example.

The camp had been so crowded with the new arrivals. It was overwhelming. Not even the treehouse was a safe haven from the noise. The new ones were also a much more violent bunch. If you know Peter, then you shouldn't be surprised by this. He always collected both the abandoned and those not quite fitting in. If they were lost, they were his to take as new crew members. Peter thought it was a fair thing to do. It was good form to take what society spits back out. A sense of pride would fill him every time, being the captain of the lost. This is why Peter felt hurt when Allison told him that she wanted to go to the beach only with Will and Dash because she viewed the others as too out of control.

Peter didn't protest her decision, he knew better than that. He could see the stress on her face and in the way she held her stance. It made his heart sink. Peter nodded. "Then I'll take you somewhere good." He took Allison by the hand and Allison took Will's hand, which the little boy already had half-extended for her to hold. Dash walked a little distantly behind them. When they got close to arriving at this good beach, Allison could smell the sea water and hear the sea gulls so much clearer. As soon as sand and the clashing blues from the water and sky were in sight, Dash separated from them to do his own thing. Will broke her gentle hold of his hand to run down the sandy bank to scare a few gulls. She half-smiled at how wildly he played. Peter mimicked her smile but couldn't help but feel concerned. "What's wrong?" he asked her.

Allison shrugged, her eyes met his and her lips drew into a line. In a moment of deliberation, she thought about so many different options, but all of which she knew could be hurtful to Peter. So, she just grinned at him and redirected her attention to Will. She mildly hopped down the sandy bank to avoid slipping and ran out to meet Will where he played. She sat down beside the little boy and picked up a shell and a smooth pebble from the sand.

"I used to collect these," she said to Will. Then she gave him the prettiest of the pebbles. He looked at it with wonder, almost like it was the first gift he ever received.

Peter smiled as he watched her and Will. He made his way to them deliberately slow. He liked the picture and lost himself in a daydream that this is what a family could be. Finally, he plopped down in the sand with them. Allison looked into his eyes, and he met her gaze with a closed-mouth grin. Each tried to judge the other. The brightness of the sun and rushing waves, the gentleness of the moment gave her just enough time to bury her concerns. But as soon as the warmth of the day turned to evening and voices floated up in the forest behind them, she was reminded of something she couldn't explain. It was an awful, empty feeling in the pit of her stomach and an aching thought in her head.

If only she could stay in that moment with Peter. Moments like this were so easy, but she couldn't help a feeling of dread. With all the new boys and the related troubles, there was exhaustion. This beach day ended with some of the new lost boys piling onto the beach, looking for mischief. She was met with deadpan stares and other behavior that they were smart enough to do when Peter's back was turned. Eventually, Allison left the beach and took Will back to camp. She tucked him in and told him he'd be alright. But she really wasn't sure if she spoke the truth. She could hear the new boys yelling in the distance, their play rougher than what she thought was morally right.

It was a mix of these things that caused her to withdraw, each day's hustle becoming a little harder to tolerate, especially since she warned Peter about his games, but the warnings were shrugged off and ignored. He'd claim the games to be good for the boys, useful for survival on the island, but Allison couldn't stop feeling sick about it. And with Benjamin away so often, a sense of loneliness weighted her in both remorse—maybe knowing deep down that he was right—and stubbornness, the wildness of Neverland exciting her too much to be well-reasoning.

The island was awake with every ounce of luxury a place like this could have. The air was tranquil and smelled of a hint of damp soil from some rain they had gotten the night prior. The sun would peak out of the clouds but disappear again. Allison was still in the treehouse, sitting on her bed, looking out at the glossy leaves that flickered when the sun made appearances. Mist coiled off the balcony, and she imagined it likely draped the forest floor. She pulled a fur blanket closer to her, tucking it tighter so it was intertwined with her legs, her fingers playing with the soft seams. The air was somewhere between warm and chilled this morning. She hadn't left the room much in the last few days. She tried telling herself that it was just the misty, rainy weather, the cold damp, the island chill. But, without actually fleshing the words out in her head, she knew better. Not quite knowing if it was this unsaid thought or the onset of more mist outside, she turned in bed so that she no longer faced the balcony. She stared at the wooden wall, unsure of how to even begin giving herself advice.

There was a quiet sound on the balcony, one that she immediately noticed to be Peter's bare feet plopping down on the wet balcony floor. She tensed slightly, only relaxing when she ceased to hear anything else. But the sound of feet brushing over the wooden floor of the bedroom caused her to stiffen again. She remained staring at the wall, wondering if her eyes should be open or closed, she didn't turn to face him. Peter's shoulders were slumped, a frown on his lips and loneliness regrettably visible in his eyes.

"You won't come out today?" Peter's voice was quiet, cautious that maybe she was still asleep.

Allison only sighed to herself, having nothing to say at the moment. She couldn't begin to explain how she felt. The only thing she knew was that she desired to be alone just a while longer. Peter's voice was lighthearted but there was a hint of sadness in it that couldn't be hid from Allison.

He tried to mask it with warmth. "You're hiding?"

A faint smile found her lips, finding his attempt at teasing her sweet but she didn't answer him. Her gaze still stayed fixed on the wooden wall, focusing on nothing in particular, just far away. He came deeper into the room slowly and almost deliberately heavy-footed. He closed more distance, making it known that he was present. He stood near the bed, looking at her back for any sign that she was conscious—he had a feeling that she was. Whether she knew it or not, her fingers played with the fabric of the blanket.

"You've been quiet lately," he said, gentle.

Her fingers paused, the hesitation giving her away. Peter moved around to her side and crouched slightly so he could be a little more eye level. His hair fell over his furrowed brows and threatened to partially cover his soft eyes. He searched her face for answers, wondering for an excruciating moment if she felt unwell.

"Hey, there…" His head tilted slightly, coaxing her to look at him. His voice was soft, hidden concern nearly choking it. "Where are you?"

Allison let a slow breath out. She wanted to vocalize, but the words were stuck and still incompletely formed, blurry even to her. Communicating words would be impossible. She turned her gaze slightly toward him, almost thinking she could manage a tiny smile. It was fleeting, reassuring a bit, but still too distant for Peter's satisfaction. His eyes narrowed, trying to get a reading on her. He knew what was going on, he just didn't want to admit it. Allison let the hurt in his eyes sink into her understanding.

"I'm here," she finally said.

Something flashed into his eyes, maybe deeper concern or maybe frustration, Allison wasn't sure what. Instead of pressing, his lips formed a crooked grin. He thought maybe a change in tactics could do the trick. Dropping down to one knee beside the bed, he rested his elbows on the fur blanket. She could feel his warm breath against her hand.

Peter forced his voice to be light and mock-accusing. "You little liar. I think you've been trying to avoid me."

Allison's lips parted and she shook her head. "I—"

"You *have*." He cut her off, leaning in just a little bit with a lazy grin. "You can't lose me so easy, you know."

The way that he looked at her made her heart flutter involuntarily. Before she could say something, she felt his hand move, gliding across the blanket to just barely brush across her knee. It lingered there, deliberately.

"I think we should get some air." His voice was teasingly low. His fingers toyed with the fabric covering her knee, and he smiled at her. "Let's play."

Allison frowned, her brows knit together, and she curled up subtly nudging his hand away. "Play?"

There was a glimmer of mischief in his eyes and his grin grew more boyishly at her guarded response. "Hide and seek, I mean." He smirked at her. "Unless…you're scared I'll win, of course."

Relaxing, she tilted her head, her lips forming a line, totally unamused. It caused his silly grin to widen all the more. He got the reaction he was craving from her. She just shook her head at him, a laugh threatening to form.

She rolled her eyes. "I *am not* scared," she said.

Peter smiled a bit darkly and rested his chin on the bed while simultaneously reaching for her hand. "Then prove it."

Allison stared at him. She weighed the invite and did her best to search his face for something she couldn't quite put her finger on. Peter lifted his head, returning her gaze. It was an unyielding, irritating gaze, but the way his lips curled up at the edges, coaxingly—it made her want to do anything he'd ask.

"But" he said, challenging her, "if you'd rather stay in our room all alone…" he leaned in and the look on his face let her know that he was up to no good.
The cockiness in his grin grew. He knew he had her right where he wanted—he did nothing to hide it in his face. Allison's lips parted as if to gasp, but nothing came out. She stared at him. Then, with a little annoyed huff, she threw the blanket off her legs without regard to it hitting him in the face. He laughed and watched her swing her legs over the side of the bed.

"Fine," she said. "But you can't make me enjoy it."

When she stood, he towered a little over her, looking into her eyes with something more. It had power over her for a moment but some chattering outside the treehouse brought her back. She blinked and moved to brush past him toward the balcony, but he reached out to her, catching her wrist and causing her to have an abrupt stop. His eyes were soft.

"I missed seeing you around," he said.

She could almost have sworn that there was a hint of reverence in his tone. Before she could think of a response, he released her and took a playful step onto the balcony. Mischief returned to his features.

"Well," he said. "Should I help you down, or can you keep up yourself?" He stepped backward to the edge of the balcony.

She hesitated. She was still thrown by the softness he had shown. Sunshine sneaked through the treetops and warmed the balcony's deck, warmly kissing their toes. Peter noticed her stance. She was strangely relaxed but tense all at the same time. He thought just at that moment that maybe a game wouldn't be best after all, but he loved games.

"How 'bout this." He snaked his arms around her. "I help you down, then I'll give you a head start."

The way his fingers rubbed little circles into her back gave her tingles all over. Lost boys were starting to pool into the yard of the treehouse—yelling and being unruly as usual. The sun was just starting to dry the leaves enough that little fairies began peeking out from their own little homes and fluttering around. She glanced up at him. He was smiling.

"Alright," she agreed.

***

Sweat. She was sweating, she couldn't believe she was sweating. The sun positioned itself in the evening sky, dipping low. Small streams of gold could be seen through the canopy of trees. Hide and seek was somehow different here than on the mainland. Stumbling over an exposed root, she started to regret accepting the invitation. The game took her farther into the jungle than she expected. She lost count of how many times the game had already been played. Each time, he won. The birds, trills, and creaky sounds were so loud, she almost couldn't think. It messed with her senses. She was shocked by it actually. Normally, Peter would hate to have her out of his sight like this. It was so playful at first. Peter had only watched for a moment, giving her a head start into the forest… She wasn't aware just how much this little game could feel like a genuine chase between hawk and rabbit. From the early morning, her heart couldn't stop rapidly beating. It seemed to get quicker from both the chase and from feeling that he was close. She could sense it.

She slowed down again, lungs nearly burning for rest. She found some refuge. Crouching behind a cluster of tangled roots, she took shallow breaths. The scent of pine wood and damp soil hung in the air so close to the cool ground. She took a daring glance over her shoulder—nothing yet. But she could feel him. She looked up into the crowns of all the trees. Birds kept darting back and forth, there wasn't anything moving larger than that. She scanned the woods, swearing that he was surely somewhere, watching with that cocky grin on his face. She shook her head, relaxing a bit into the roots.

She murmured under her breath, teasing herself for building the game up to be more heart-racing than it probably was. "You're imagining things," she said.

"Are you?" Peter's voice was low, sounding disembodied and creeping somewhere through the trees.

Allison gasped. Her spine stiffened, even her pulse seemed to hitch. Spinning around so that her back was to the roots, her eyes narrowed. There wasn't anything there, just teasing chuckles up in the branches. It was playful but *off.*

"You're cheating." Her voice was breathless.

His voice was smooth and hidden. "Oh, but you never set the rules."

A sudden gust of shadow swept through the leaves, and she nearly screamed just as he dropped from a low branch behind her—soundlessly. He was crouched down, eyes gleaming at her through the tangled roots. She stood and stumbled out from her hiding place, but his arms were around her faster than she could turn to escape. He was grinning, his grip tightening.

"Hey!" She half-laughed and half-gasped, wriggling slightly from the proximity.

"Gotcha." He teased.

He closed more proximity by just a fraction. His breath was warm against her throat. Allison paused, her hand finding his chest after feeling the faintest graze of his lips against her skin. It wasn't a kiss but a promise of one to come. He lingered there, inhaling her scent, an action that sent a wave of chills down her body. Her fingers twitched against his chest, torn between pulling him closer or pushing him away…

She swallowed. "You were supposed to give me more of a head start this time."

Peter chuckled, gripping her closer, his nose and eyes lashes tickling her. "Hmm. I did. You're just too easy to catch." His lips moved to her ear, practically forcing her head to tilt, voice just slightly above a whisper. "You breathe loud when you're excited."

The faint vibration of his words made her stomach twist but not just from thrill. Peter's voice was playful, but something lingered behind it. His arms were still closed around her, maybe too possessively. Adrenaline made his eyes glow with unwavering focus. Allison let an airy laugh out, not really because anything was funny.

"You always have to win?" She tested him.

He pulled away just enough to eye her. "When the prize is worth it."

Her breath hitched and for a short moment, her hands lingered more deliberately on his chest. She didn't know if she wanted to finally push away, ensure that nothing could go too far. The forest grew darker and there was thunder rumbling in the distance. A stillness crept. His eyes searched hers, unrelentingly wild, a spark in them made her feel something that no other guy ever made her feel before. She couldn't look away from him and he knew it.

His voice was low and knowing. "You're not scared of me… are you?"

Her lips parted to give an answer, but before she could try, a sharp voice cut through the stillness. It caused her to jerk in Peter's arms, the spell slowly withering between them.

"Get off him!" Another distant angry shout came.

Peter's hands were slow to release her, his eyes were locked on hers, searching for something she couldn't identify. All too suddenly, the tension snapped. The voices grew in number—angrier, violent—closing in. A blur of a scuffle near the distant tree line caught their attention. Three of the lost boys could be seen struggling, a circle of other boys formed around them, each yelling.

Peter stepped forward; eyes focused on the commotion. He turned his head slightly towards Allison who was behind him. "Stay." He told her.

Then he flew ahead, swiftly and effortlessly like a ghost. Of course, Allison had no intention of listening to Peter's demand. She hurried to catch up. One of the boys shoved the other hard against a log. A sloppy punch was thrown but it missed. Leaves scattered and voices snarled with increasingly murderous intent. It was the kind of cold, hardened fight that smelled of reckless brute strength and rivalry. She reached Peter.

Her eyes widened from the scene, her voice uncertain. "What—"

Before she could finish, Peter's arm extended, bumping her, to keep her from stepping any further. He was protective but not gentle, almost instinctively territorial. His body stiffened. The easygoingness and charm in his eyes hardened. It took her a second time reviewing the situation for her to realize it. He wasn't moving to stop the fight, he was watching it—closely, calculating—as if waiting to see a specific outcome.

His voice was calm, dangerously calm, eyes fixed on the brawl. "Stay behind me…"

Shaking her head in defiance, Allison pushed past Peter and a few other boys brutally cheering the fight. It happened too quickly for Peter to stop. She yelled at one of the boys whose fists were relentlessly striking the other. Grabbing the striker's arm, he turned to her and in one violent motion, he shifted and sent a strike with the back of his hand, flinging her to the ground with a harsh thud. Before she could shake the ringing from her ears, the striker's attention was wholly on her.

This violence wasn't the first time… ever since this new batch of lost boys came to the island, everything was more dangerous. Peter tried to control them, but it never stopped fights like this. They only grew more rebellious, more vicious. They begrudged Peter's rules; they hated Allison's attempt to care.

The striker loomed over her, wide-eyed with ideas. But in a split second, Peter was behind him, burying a dagger in the striker's ribs. Peter pulled the dagger free in one smooth motion, his movements disturbingly effortless. His eyes flickered back to Allison—softening into boyish concern, as if violence had never even touched him. The striker fell, barely missing where she lay, causing her to gasp. Peter's eyes were on her, always, half-afraid and half...*satisfied.* In that brief moment, she realized what Benjamin was warning her about. Peter's easy charm, his playful crooked grin could all fade away too easily, revealing something far less tame beneath.

Chapter Sixteen

The intensity of the lost boys only worsened. It got so bad that she was kept within the boundaries of the treehouse, again. It was for her own protection, that's what Peter said. Each day he would only leave the treehouse to bring fresh food and water or perhaps a surprise. They had spent each night since the fight curled up together, talking. Mostly, Allison would just listen to him recall past stories. She was certain that most of them were untrue but anything to fill the silence and monotonous of the day was welcome. She tried to study him differently than before—watching more carefully for what excited him, and if there were ever any signs of remorse. She couldn't tell. Allison thought she hid her new wariness of Peter, but he knew something had changed. She was always tense in his arms now, withdrawn. It burned into him with unforgiving vigor. Peter knew his actions (or lack thereof) caused her silence. He just didn't know how to fix it. He didn't have a choice. Threats had to be dealt with, one way or another. He did nothing wrong. The fact that he knew that Allison thought he had made him close to bitter. But he had no choice, he would need to make it up to her—earn trust again.

He was lying in bed with her, watching her sleep. Her closed eyes were beautifully decorated by long lashes and her hair was messily fanned across the pillow. Her lips were parted almost teasingly. The memory of moments before the fight flickered in front of his mind. The desperate desire to have her so close again, her pulse under his lips, gave his eyes a new glint of darkness. He had to do something to make a moment like that return.

Peter left the treehouse before Allison woke. She knew by the missing weight at her side that he was already gone. She opened her eyes and glanced around the room, surprised to find him gone. Lying on her back for a moment, she turned her head to look outside. It was an overcast day, which turned the whole island several shades greener, and it was all the easier to spot fairies and hear birds that are normally quieter. It was a very still morning. She took a second to inhale, feeling good because she had some time to herself no matter how brief. Tossing the covers aside and slipping out of bed, she took her time combing her hair and selecting a homemade dress. She even took a seashell and fastened it in her hair. She stood in front of the mirror, sighing at the fact that there was nothing she could do to cover the freckling.

She looked herself hard in the eyes. *It's okay*, she thought. It felt important to think up as many positive affirmations as possible. Peter never did anything to hurt her. He only ever wanted to keep her safe. She felt guilty. There was no need for it, feeling that way about Peter. She saw that side of him, the side that maybe enjoyed violence but there was another side, too. And that side wanted love, wanted attention, affection—it was a protective side that she knew deep down was meant only for her. She had to have faith that things would work out for the best. The lost boys would somehow find a way to be peaceful, and the island would become her own personal paradise. Still watching the mirror, she ghosted her fingertips over the places that Peter had almost kissed. She wished he had. Her mind reminisced, cycling through all the things she could have done to encourage it. She imagined herself having leaned in more or maybe tilting her head…or not having been so afraid to look deeper into his eyes, to touch him.

She walked to the balcony and beheld the island, feeling much like a tropical Juliet. Then, she smiled fondly. Will knelt in the sand playing with pebbles that he likely collected from the shore. Her smile faded just a little bit from a sudden daydream about wishing that she had been with Will while he collected the pebbles. He was, after all, such a small boy and she worried that he was always in danger. This wariness caused her to almost call out to him. She was sure that she could convince Peter to let the little boy stay with them in the treehouse until things settled down. But Will was playing so content that she made the foolish motherly mistake of giving him a little more free-time. It would have been better had she called for him earlier. Another boy, no older than Will—new to the island—appeared in the corner of Allison's vision. He, too, was so little that she forgot to be worried. It wasn't until Will was suddenly lying flat down on top of his pebble collection that she turned her attention to the excited shrieks of the other boy and noticed the old-fashioned slingshot in his raised hand.

It was one of those awful moments when she just couldn't force her hands free from the balcony rail—her knuckles turning white. When she finally freed her hands, it seemed like her feet couldn't move fast enough to climb down from the balcony. As soon as she was close to the ground, she jumped the rest of the way and rushed to Will's side. Her knees hit the ground and, already in tears, hesitantly touched the boy and said his name as if trying to gently wake him. She knew he was dead. The other boy sprinted to Allison and asked proudly if he had killed the coyote. Allison forced her tears aside and removed the coyote-skin hood from Will's head. A look of terror sent the little killer into a panicky state of bawling.

Allison cried until Peter arrived. She mourned Will's death but also mourned for the new boy, knowing what Peter would do once he found out. Crying was always something Peter hated to see. The mere sound of it awakened something too close to reality in him, almost as if the sound reminded him he would never be safe from the consequences of mortality. It was seeing Allison so deeply distraught that sent him beyond the state of reasoning. He flew at them, his darkened eyes taking in the scene. He saw the body and the slingshot in the other boy's hand. Peter didn't even speak; he didn't need to ask questions. Peter's jaw tensed and he raised his fist to strike the boy hard, but Allison screamed and begged mercy for the boy.

Peter's lip curled. "Go inside…"

She sobbed, grabbing his raised arm. "He's just a little boy. Peter they can't tell the difference!"

Peter noted the remorse in the new boy's face. Peter turned to look at Allison. He couldn't bear to see her upset, so he dropped his hand and forced his fist to relax. By this time, some of the other lost boys appeared and lowered their hoods. Among them were Dash and Benjamin who stared at the scene in near disbelief. Benjamin stepped forward first and knelt next to Will, then looking at Peter for permission, he lifted Will's body to go bury him.   Allison met Benjamin's sorry glance, something in it nearly killing her. She knew that they wouldn't waste time putting him in the ground. The image of no casket made her queasy. She sat on the ground and cried out loud. It frightened the younger lost boys and made the older ones anxious because they could see how angry it was making Peter.

Peter tried to comfort her, but she fought him off and hugged her own knees. Finally, her refusal caused Peter to yell at the lost boys, insisting that they all go away, and they did. Once Benjamin took Will's body out of her sight and Peter and Allison were left alone, she leapt to her feet and ran into the forest. Peter stood there, frozen.

***

The island was suddenly and strangely quiet. The usual bustle of distant laughter was gone and the rustling of the leaves was absent. It was as though the trees themselves were even grieving. The air, once warm and welcoming, felt cold despite the lingering humidity, especially with a stormy wind sweeping up from the coast. She didn't know how long she had been running. Allison sat on a mossy boulder near the edge of the clearing, her arms wrapped tightly around herself, rocking slightly, as if trying to hold in the tremors rattling her. Her eyes were red and puffy, and her breath came in short, broken sobs. Seemingly countless moments passed before she looked up from her knees toward the sea. The breeze threaded through her hair, stinging her tearstained cheeks. She felt Peter's presence before she saw him, his warmth at her back like the promise of sunlight after rain, yet it was tainted. He knelt beside her, his hand firm but gentle on her knee. She didn't look at him.

"It's my fault," she choked, her voice strangled with guilt.

Her hands were damp with tears as she covered her face again. She rocked forward slightly, her thoughts splintering back to Benjamin's warnings—the soft, grave warnings she had brushed off. She had been so foolish. Peter's jaw clenched, and he quickly cupped her face with both hands, pulling her tear-streaked gaze to his. His eyes were wild, gleaming with an intensity she couldn't place—anger, sorrow, desperation.

"No," he said hoarsely. "No. It is not your fault."

His thumb stroked her cheekbone, wiping at her tears as if trying to erase her grief.

Her body stilled. A shadow of decisiveness crossed her face, sharp and certain. She met his eyes—calm, but terribly firm.

"I think," she hesitated, her voice barely above a whisper.

Her lip trembled slightly. Peter's throat tightened. He suddenly knew what she was going to say before she said it, but he willed her not to.

Her eyes glimmered with fragile resolve. "We should go home."

His hands fell from her face. For the first time in a long while, Peter froze in a way that felt like he was on the brink of something dangerous. A moment of silence clung to the cooling air. His eyes searched hers, but she didn't back down.

"You're just tired and sad," he said, forcing a small, unconvincing smile. His fingers curled lightly around hers, pressing her palm to his chest as if he could steady her trembling.

"Tomorrow, I'll take you to the other side of the island, and we will be far away from the lost boys." He tucked a strand of her dampened hair behind her ear and rashly pressed his lips to her temple. She closed her eyes and swallowed, trying desperately to soak up the imprint of his lips before the kiss disappeared. "You'll forget this. We'll find a new place. Just us."

She pulled back slightly, biting back desire, and hiccupped against her tears. Her eyes were pleading now, wide and shining with desperation. She turned to him and clung to his shirt, fisting the fabric weakly.

"Peter... I can't keep seeing this violence," she whispered brokenly.

He flinched at the words. His expression hardened slightly. He jerked her to her feet, a little rougher than he meant to. His fingers dug into her waist. "The mainland is violent, too," he countered, his voice lower now—dangerous in its calmness. "Out there, you will see blood on the streets. You will hear screams in the night. You think you can escape it?" He shook his head slightly. "The real world is not the dream you remember."

Her chin trembled. "I want to go back." Her throat tightened. "I swear... I'll never do anything stupid again."

For a moment, she let herself imagine the world she had left behind—the normal one. She thought of her old life, the faces of people she had once known. Then her thoughts drifted to Benjamin, Dash, and the other lost boys—the way they were slipping further from themselves. Hollowing. Fading. They were the ones losing their minds here, day by day.

Her voice strengthened. "And the lost boys will come with me."

Peter's arms slackened. His hold on her faltered. His expression darkened into something hard and sharp. His eyes, once tender, glimmered with a dangerous flash of possession.

He released her so suddenly that she nearly fell backward. He turned his back to her, pressing his hands against his face, fingers digging into his temples as though trying to crush what was starting to waken inside him. His breaths came in slow, heavy bursts.

"If you go back," he rasped through clenched teeth, "you'll grow old and die someday and be stuck in the ground to rot. You *want* that?"

Her voice, though small, was steady. "People die here, too, Peter."

His eyes narrowed. His hands fell to his sides, curling into fists. His breath was sharp and quick, and he spun back to face her, his voice rising. "Not if you know how to beat it," he snapped. He stepped toward her, voice low and fervent. "I will teach you. Alice, it is wrong for you to leave."

She staggered back slightly, staring at him. Her lips parted slightly, but no words came. She let out a slow breath and shook her head faintly.

Her voice was barely audible. "It's wrong for me to stay."

For the first time, she saw something splinter in his eyes. His mouth quivered slightly, and for a heartbeat, she thought he might cry. But he didn't. Instead, he exhaled slowly, deliberately, and his face went emotionless.

His voice was void of warmth now. "Alright," he said flatly. "But the lost boys stay with me." His stare sharpened, glinting with an ominous promise. His voice lowered into a quiet, lethal growl. "And I warn you... it will be worse for them if you go."

Her stomach turned, blood running cold. She blinked once, twice—staring into his eyes, searching for the boy she saw on Dandelion Hill. But all she saw was a quiet, simmering wrath—a festering rage just below the surface. Peter blamed the lost boys now. She could feel it—the resentment in his voice. It was their fault, in his mind, that she wanted to leave. If she abandoned him, he would surely thin them out. She wanted to believe he was bluffing, that his threats were nothing more than a wounded heart lashing out. But deep down, something raw and instinctive—the part of her that had learned to read the glint in his eyes—knew he wasn't.

She felt her breath hitch. When she imagined the faces of Benjamin, Dash, and the other lost boys, her throat constricted. Her fingers curled into trembling fists at her sides. She couldn't stand the thought of leaving them to Peter's anger. Her voice, quiet and broken, barely carried over the rising wind.

"Please... don't hurt them," she whispered.

He stared at her, unmoving. His jaw was tight. He didn't answer. Instead, he simply turned and walked away, leaving her standing in the clearing with nothing but the scent of coastal earth and the lingering weight of his unspoken threat. His silhouette blurred against the rising mist of warm ground and cool air, and each of his footsteps thudded dully against the wet earth until she couldn't hear him anymore.

Chapter Seventeen

If you know the feeling of tiptoeing past a sleeping dog that has a mean streak, then you know a small percentage of how Allison feels. She didn't say yes to staying but she didn't say no either because she neither wanted to lie or appear stubborn. It was awful the lead he took when dealing with the lost boys, it seemed like half of the new lost boys disappeared overnight. Whether Peter was responsible for that is debatable, but the effect is certain, those left over were mechanical in their responses to Peter. They would always salute him as captain and didn't so much as chase a rabbit without his approval.

At this point, Allison was allowed out of the treehouse and returned to her responsibilities. The lost boys were very cautious around her and always had to address her kindly and stand up whenever she entered their presence. That was the rule. She actually hated it fiercely because she knew the true look behind almost every lost boy's eyes, a look of resentment—that glint she learned to recognize in Peter. It was really all the same, just at different levels of cleverness. She never did stop thinking about going home; a place that settled a little more sweetly in her memory now. After a while, she daydreamed of it the same way that she used to daydream of disappearing to a magical world separate from reality. She smiled one late evening and watched the fairies and the little trail of flying dust that they sometimes left behind and it gave her a perfectly splendid idea.

Fetching a little glass bottle from one of the many small trunks in the treehouse, she checked to see if anyone was watching, then she leaned over the balcony railing and swept the fairy dust into the bottle. It was a very small amount, but after days of collecting it, the dust collection grew very plentiful. The trick of course was keeping the sparkling bottle hidden from Peter. Over time, she believed that she could collect enough for all the lost boys to join in leaving Neverland but the one she wanted most to leave with her was Benjamin.

***

The morning air smelled damp and fresh from last night's rain. The sun was still straining to get through the canopy of trees, illuminating the waterdrops that clung to the leaves like diamonds. This was the morning when she believed that she might have enough of the dust.

With trembling fingers and held breath, she cradled the two bottles of fairy dust. The glass was cool and smooth in her palm, the delicate shimmer inside catching faint light like she had managed to bottled stars.

Her pulse quickened—partly from emotional excitement, partly from fear of being caught. She knelt by one of the wooden trunks, her heart pounding with each creak that the floorboards made beneath her knees. Her hands, clumsy and unsteady, felt around the contents of the trunk, but she managed to wedge one of the bottles deep beneath layers of unfolded fabric, loose paper, and other forgotten things. She tucked it away far enough that only the most persistent of hands could ever find it. She pressed the other bottle against her chest, then hid it on her person. With a last glance around the room, she tiptoed onto the balcony. Her knuckles whitened as she gripped the railing. Her eyes swept over the treetops, frantically searching for him.

Nothing. No flash of any white smile. No shadow soaring against the clouds. He had been cold and distant since the day of the Will's death. His smiles had become brittle and hollow. The warmth she had once sought in them was gone, replaced by something colder, more possessive. But his anger served her well now—because she couldn't feel his presence. He was nowhere in sight.

Without wasting any more time, she swung a leg over the balcony railing and climbed down from the treehouse. The bark dug into her palms as she tried to hurry, too impatient today for caution. She landed with a mushy thud on the damp forest floor and took off running. The forest was alive with the trill of birds and the distant rustle of unseen creatures, but she barely heard any of it. Her breaths came in short bursts as she raced through the woods. The branches clawed at her arms, leaves snagged in her hair, but she didn't care. She smiled thinking about Benjamin's hideaway. Her heart leapt when she came to the familiar clearing.

When she reached the hollowed tree, her hands shook slightly as she brushed away the loose ferns, exposing the hidden lid. With one last glance over her shoulder, she pulled it open and lowered herself down the narrow tunnel. The damp scent of earth and old parchment filled her senses again.

"Benjamin!" she whispered sharply, her voice carrying through the stillness.

A figure emerged from the dim candlelight. His eyes were wide with concern— the deep brown darker in the low light. His hair was mussed, falling in wild strands over his forehead, and there was ink smudged on the edge of his hand.

"Allison," he said, voice low with worry as he scanned her face, surprised to see her. "What is it?"

But her bright smile dissolved the tension in his eyes instantly. The lines on his face softened, and when she held up the glowing bottle of fairy dust, his lips parted in disbelief.

Her voice barely contained her breathless excitement.

"I have it." She swallowed hard. "Two bottles."

He blinked, stunned, then slowly grinned. A boyish, disbelieving grin—the kind she hadn't seen in weeks. It was enough to make her throat tighten with emotion. Without a word, he closed the distance between them. His hands hovered over the bottle, almost afraid to touch it.

"Where? How? Peter never lets anyone collect this. How did you even learn about it"

"I don't know. The fairies are covered in it. I thought that maybe—"

"Your thoughts are correct!" he said softly, voice hoarse with a mixture of hope and disbelief.

She squeezed his hand briefly, her fingers warm against his. "Then, we can leave."

For a moment, he didn't speak. His gaze softened, and his breath came in an uneven, shaky exhale, as though he were afraid to believe it. His lips twitched slightly at the edges, almost laughing. "Yes, yes!" Then he let out a soft, incredulous chuckle. "You are mad," he whispered, eyes gleaming. "Perfectly mad!"

She laughed with him. It was a laugh that made her feel free for the first time in what felt like forever. The sound filled the tiny room with warmth. She grabbed his wrist, practically dragging him toward the tunnel.

"Come on," she urged breathlessly. "We can plan the whole thing—we'll find the lost boys and—"

"Wait," he said, halting her with a hand on her arm.

Her brow furrowed, confused. But when she turned, she saw the warmth in his eyes—the brightness she hadn't seen in so long. A shared glimmer of hope. Then an important question came to her mind.

"How do we use it?" she asked, barely able to contain her eagerness.

He smiled and placed his hand on her back to guide her upward, steadying her as she climbed. His palm was warm, grounding her. When they both emerged into the sun-speckled forest, she turned to face him, breathless. He leaned closely like he was about to tell a secret.

"Well…" he smirked slightly. "We think about good things."

Her eyes widened slightly, breath catching. "Good things?"

His eyes held hers. "Things that make us happy."

She blinked, then laughed. Her laugh was full, genuine, and bright—a sound so rare these days that it caught them both off guard.

"That should be easy now more than ever," she grinned, her eyes sparkling with sudden lightness.

For a brief, fleeting moment, the island seemed less suffocating. But the happy moment, that taste for eventual freedom, died when Allison's eyes caught a glimpse of movement in the forest. She froze, eyes meeting something that would ruin everything. Benjamin's smile faded upon glancing in the direction of Allison's stare. It was Peter. Motionless, he stood in the half-shadowed light, watching them with a stillness that made the blood in her veins stop cycling. He appeared in front of them like magic, likely a more realistic taste of how fast his flight could be. She looked up into Peter's darkened, dangerous expression. Her breath caught.

The glow of the fading sun behind clouds clung to his face, painting his sharp cheekbones in streaks of gold and shadow. His eyes were distant and seething and, in his hand, he clutched with deliberate cruelty, the bottle of fairy dust she had hidden in the treehouse. The soft golden light of it seemed delicate, but in his hand, it was a weapon.

She staggered forward, her voice breaking.

"Peter… I—" But the words faltered, sticking to her throat. He said nothing. His eyes just roamed over her face, aching.

Benjamin stepped in front of her. Peter's eyes narrowed, unblinking. His head tilted and he prowled forward, circling them with calculated steps—silent, but utterly ruinous. He held up the bottle, turning it slowly between his fingers, eyes not leaving Allison. His lips curled into a cruel imitation of a smile, but his eyes were dead.

"Whose idea?" Peter asked softly—too softly. It was the voice of a man on the edge of something terrible. His gaze never left Allison.

"Whose. Idea?" He repeated, almost like a whisper.

Benjamin stepped more protectively in front of her. "Mine."

Peter blinked, once and slowly. Then he exhaled sharply through his nose, and his chest heaved with the force of it.

"You." He hissed, his voice shaking. He stared at Benjamin as though seeing him for the first time as a true challenger. His hands trembled slightly. "You did it." His breath came in ragged pulls. "Why?"

But he didn't need the answer. He already knew. He let out a broken sound, a choked laugh, so bitter that it made her stomach twist. Then, for a moment, it seemed like he blocked them out. Allison used this moment of Peter's silent rage to order Benjamin to run, pleading with him to take the younger lost boys into hiding as well as himself. Poor Benjamin, the hardest thing that any good boy could ever do is leave a damsel in distress, but he knew that she was still the safest one on this wretched island, so he did what she wanted and left as quickly as he could. Allison watched Benjamin vanish into the woods and she imagined him beginning to gather all the little lost boys that she loved like her own so that they could be safe.

Without warning, Peter closed the distance between them. Before Allison could react, he threw the bottle. It exploded against a tree with a burst of light, sending dust glittering like dying stars through the air.

"No!" she screamed, reaching for him, but he shoved her back with one hand, his strength overwhelming. She stumbled, landing hard on her palms.

"Where's the other?" His voice was low and menacing, but his eyes were wild and desperate.

She shook her head, tears in her eyes. "I—there's no other!"

"Don't lie."

A silence stretched between them. Her pulse was pounding in her ears, but she found the courage to stand and walk toward him. He was still for a moment, seething and watching her move in front of him. Her goal was to distract him—to try desperately to hide the fear in her eyes and replace it with love—to coax him into going back to camp or back to the treehouse. It almost seemed like it would work. He looked at her, and for a fleeting moment, something softer—something pained—passed through his eyes. And then, with a savage snarl, he lunged past her toward the tree. She was stunned from the force he used. Even her palms were still burning from the first time he had pushed her, though she really didn't notice it much. She was locked on him, his anger. When he approached the tree that marked

Benjamin's hideaway, his knees struck the ground. With trembling hands, he opened the hidden door.

"No, wait!" She scrambled to reach him, but he didn't look at her, didn't hesitate. He disappeared into the opened entrance and down the tunnel. "No!" She called out again, lunging to reach him. But she was too slow. She followed, skidding down the tunnel.

When she reached the bottom of the tunnel, he was there standing in the middle of the room. In that moment, he was completely quiet and frozen. Then, he started to look around. He began to move, walking like someone in deep consideration on the brink of losing control. His bare feet kicked up the neatly swept dirt floor as he crossed the room. Peter's fingers brushed over the book spines, his eyes skimming over the scattered pages and pieces of freshly written-on parchment. He glanced over the short messy notes, the long deliberate sentences, and the things he was barred from understanding.

He turned and faced the desk, picking up one of the journals. Allison's throat tightened, recognizing it as the one with Benjamin's father's image in it. He flipped through the pages, tracing his thumb over the edge of the page he chose to stop at. His eyes narrowed for a moment at the image, something flashing in his eyes, but it faded. His attention scanned the words, all those meaningless scribbles and symbols, all lovely and mocking in their foreignness to him. He inhaled, and the breath hitched. There was too much that he couldn't understand and the weight of it felt like betrayal. His eyes lifted from the journal and drifted across the rest of the room. Everything was filled with pages, quills, and ink—all out of his reach, out of his control.

He shuddered. "You want me to do awful things," Peter said, his face paled.

A prickling chill crept down her spine like icy little spiders.

"No, Peter," Her voice was shaking now, "Good things. I want you to do good things."

"The lost boys," he said, without looking at her. "They haven't hurt you, did they? Don't they listen to you and respect you now that there are only obedient boys left. Don't I respect you, Allison? Do you not feel safe?"

Her silence was all the answer he needed. With a wicked grin, the journal in his hand was sent flying across the room and against the wall with a harsh crack, splitting open in midair, the pages bursting like feathers. His breathing grew more uneven. With one swift savage motion, he grabbed the edge of the homemade desk and overturned it with a pained roar. Books and loose pages hit the ground with a weighted thud. Glass shattered and ink bottles spilled and pooled in the dirt.

The candles violently flickered, the flames sputtering and struggling to stay lit against the sudden breeze as he swung his arm across the shelves. It sent journals crashing to the ground. Then, he beat his fists against the wall—one, two, three. Harder and harder until his knuckles turned red and blood smeared on the wall.

"Stop it!" Allison cried, still frozen in the entrance of the room.

He couldn't stop. He turned his attention back to the little wooden bookshelf. His eyes consumed with rage. With one powerful kick, Peter sent it crashing, splintering against the floor. Wood and ripped paper all littered the once tidy floor. The beautifully written memories practically destroyed, nothing but strewn ruins.

"Stop!" she cried again, her voice breaking. She lunged toward him, wrapping her arms around his waist from behind. She held onto him with everything she had, her nails digging into his sides. "Please!"

Peter staggered just a little from her weight, no different than a bear would struggle from a cub. He didn't yield. Instead, his hands clenched into fists. His chest heaved under her tight hold. She could feel him shaking.

"You were going to leave." His voice was low and hoarse.

Her grip on him tightened, her nails pinching into his skin even more. "I wasn't—I swear I wasn't—"

"LIAR!"

He spun around so violently that she was wrenched from him. She stumbled, hardly catching her balance against the opposite wall. She watched him with widened eyes. His chest rose and fell. His eyes filled with disbelief. Still, he visually trembled. Peter gazed at the destroyed room, at all the stories that Benjamin had preserved but never shared—stories he could never read, never know for himself. It unraveled him at his very core.

"You were going to leave me," he said again. His words were barely above a whisper, but the anguish in them was sharp enough to slice bone.

She shook her head intensely, gasping, tears streaking down her face though she tried not to. "No, I—"

But he was already turning away from her. Peter staggered to the middle of the ruins. Though his hands still trembled, he grabbed a handful of torn pages. He held them briefly, not even looking at them, but crushed them in his fists. He sank to his knees, hands still fisting the papers, blood and ink mixed together on his skin. His shoulders heaving from his breaths. For the first time he truly looked broken. The traits of anger and possessiveness so briefly gone. His eyes finally lifted to hers, reddened but still riddled with disbelief. He never really thought that she would do that to him.

"You were going to leave me," he whispered. Then there was nothing.

Her heart broke. Allison couldn't find the right words to say. He was so lost, and she knew it. She sniffled and wiped her eyes. So carefully, she approached him. Kneeling down, she hesitantly touched his wrist.

"I'm sorry, Peter."

He looked at her. "Don't ever do this again," he said. His voice was quiet, his eyes empty. He grabbed her wrist and dragged her with him back up the tunnel. The fresh breeze struck them—a rebirth for him but something so different for her.

***

There was no use in fighting him anymore. He had picked her up in his arms and flew back to the treehouse. As soon as they made it to the balcony, he released her. She crossed her arms, suddenly chilled by the air. He then did something that made her whole mind and spirit twist with contradiction. He flew to her, looking into her eyes sorrowfully—an apology lingering somewhere. Lifting her again, he found the bed. He buried his face in the crook of her neck and lay securely beside her, caging her between his arms. His breathing became relaxed, and he was asleep before she could register this side of him. Allison spent this time still fighting back tears, staring at the rustic ceiling and for the first time in a long time, she prayed. Unseen by her, a little fairy hovered in the misted light—his heart tugged by a sorrow he barely understood. And somewhere deep in the shadows of Neverland, a new thread of fate quietly began to weave.

Chapter Eighteen

Peter was frozen in sleep but every unconscious, unmoving part of him yearned to wake. It started out almost warm. Flashing images, dark and smeared, flooded the place in his mind where dreams breed. He heard a woman's voice, too distorted to understand. There was a man's voice, too—angry. The dream turned cold. He couldn't make the scene out, but it felt familiar, like it had truly happened. The voices argued and then…silence. There was a sense of decay, and he could hear tears. A weight pressed into the blur and something called to Peter, something ticked.

Peter stirred from the dream, waking earlier than usual—maybe because he was somehow more sensitive to Allison's labored breathing. His lashes fluttered, eyes and mind still heavy from sleep and the distancing visions. The soft rhythm of her breathing filled the treehouse. The lantern on the far shelf flickered for the last time before the morning sun could stretch into their room. His arm draped over her waist, pinning her close. He could feel the faint rise and fall of her ribs beneath his palm, the unevenness in her breath. His eyes fully opened, sleep sliding from him. Slowly, the memory of the previous day rose and set prominently in the forefront of his mind. Her breath fell in shallow puffs against his collarbone. He sighed noting how soft and warm she was pressed against him. She was deep in sleep, briefly unaware. He shifted to his side so that he propped himself on his elbow. He did it so carefully so she wouldn't wake up. His eyes began to study her. How her brows were still creased just a little bit. He hesitated but eventually gave in to the desire to brush his fingers over the tear trails that had dried in the night.

His ears were continuously drawn to her breathing. There was a faint rasp in it, maybe hoarse from the way he remembered her screaming at him. Peter's chest tightened uncomfortably from the memory. His fingers twitched slightly against her, but he remained close, despite being hurt by her. He closed a little more space until his lips were next to her temple. He breathed her in, and she softly stirred, exhaling a faint little sound—practically inaudible if he hadn't been so close. He held her a little closer, something that had become instinctive. His nose and forehead nuzzled her hair. He didn't really mean to do it, but it happened, and he paused in that moment. He almost liked her better this way, limp and receptive, her shoulder tucking against his chest as he held her—so warm. Though his eyes were heavy in the grayish blue light of the early morning, he refused to close his eyes. He just watched her instead.

He noted her beauty, the way her hair covered the pillow like soft waterfalls, her pink lips, and dark lashes, all features he wished dearly to freeze in time. He seemed to remember a story he heard before, involving a girl and eternal sleep. He had half a mind to search far and wide for a magical spinning wheel so that with one prick, she would sleep forever on his bed.

He understood determination. It was perhaps what he fears most with the exception of his own determination, which he views as wholly right and reasonable. But he just couldn't understand her form of determination, this terrible desire to return to a place where things are temporary. He wished she would see—*truly* see—that he was only trying to save her. He imagined the various things he could do to keep her happily on the island, but then he recalled all the places he had already shown her—and the sweetness he had given. None of it really seemed to matter—it never did with anyone.

A thought occurred and the more he stared at her, the more his mind struggled with terrible things. It was just a notion, a shadow of something he never really entertained before. Why did he need to be so afraid. Without the fairy dust, she could never go. Now that he knew that she had the patience to collect it, he would simply ensure that it didn't happen again. One way or another, she wouldn't dare. So, what if he just kept her? The thought of it made him a little ill. He never considered keeping a girl on the island if she didn't want to stay. But this time was different. There had been others before her. But no one had been her. He was so sick, so broken, so exhausted by the thought of one more leaving him. He had tried to be sweet. He tried to show all of them how beautiful and careless life could be. But mermaids, fairies, and adventure—all the beautiful things the mainland could never offer—seemed trivial after a while. It frightened him.

The faces of those before Allison were already starting to blur, becoming less and less important. He couldn't quite remember the features; he just remembered the leaving. The distance of their eyes, the desire for the mainland. It was the way they'd start telling him about when they'd go back to their lives as if forgetting all the awful things. They loved their families, they loved their memories, they loved their boring educations, even their books. They were all blinded by the glow of the status quo. They all left him and every time, he would let them go. It was a bitter thing for Peter to swallow. None of them ever seemed to understand the consequence of their choice. He watched her continue to sleep. He thought this time would be different; he was so sure.

She was different, she was like him, he had been so sure.

Then, a sinking feeling swallowed his heart and pushed it down to his stomach. Doubt nearly strangled him now. The last day, seeing her standing there with Benjamin. How they smiled together thinking they could get away from sharing in something that he couldn't also share. And he felt it again, the familiar prick of betrayal and abandonment. He had seen it in her. Even now in her sleep. He felt almost sure that she dreamed of home. It was perhaps an unmistakable truth pressing him. She would leave, just like the others, someday—that awful determination. If he didn't stop her, she'd be gone. He'd lose her to life's lie. His teeth clenched. Maybe he just wouldn't give her a choice. He threatened her once; he'd threaten her again—drag a lost boy out in front of her and kill him each and every time she tried to leave. It tasted so wrong at first but the longer it lingered, the more right it seemed. In the end, she would be saved. The pain of old age could never touch her. She would never feel loss, never feel caged here like she would in her world.

He stared at her. With the morning sun starting to peek inside the room, the glow made it easier to see the soft curve of her neck. Light blue veins were so visible in this light, soft and easily bruised. A stab of guilt punctured his chest. His hold relaxed and his fingers brushed over the bruises with reverent touches. Still, the thought of what happened didn't leave his mind. He could keep her on the island. There were always ways—things he knew. She'd no longer be haunted, not by her town, not by her family… her past. He could make her forget them all.

He could bind her to him. She would wake up each morning thinking about nothing else but him. She'd never want to leave, the longing in her eyes belonging only to him. Then, she'd always be perfect, always young— exactly how he wanted, how he needed her to be. Peter just barely caressed the cross around her neck. She'd always be alive. But as suddenly as the idea appealed to him, it turned against him with a sharp realization. It wouldn't be her anymore. Maybe it would just be a shadow, a ghost. No fire, no real passion, no game. She wouldn't be real. Somewhere in his heart, he knew fear could never replace love. His throat clenched and he curled against her, nuzzling her hair again as if her scent could make the doubt go away. It didn't.

He propped himself up again, looking at her with more desperation and unrest tightening his face. He visually traced her breakable features, every curve. His hands pressed against the soft place just above her tummy and between her ribs, feeling her flesh rise and fall. He was suddenly torn somewhere between gentleness and possessiveness. The hand soaking up her warmth flexed against her. A part of him wanted to follow through with the first plan—he could force her—but another part of him knew that she might never forgive him. Maybe she'd hate him, close herself off from him forever. If she were too strong willed… But what choice did he have? It would destroy him if she left. What made it worse is that he doubted she could ever make the flight herself and survive, so he'd have to escort her. The thought killed him, it killed him! Lying with her in the golden glow, watching her move so slightly in her slumber, he battled with what would be worse. Just how far would he go. As he thought about it, he had another idea—a third option.

There was a way to prove the awfulness of the mainland, but it was risky. He would go to the mainland and make it an unwelcoming place. Then he would return to Neverland.

Suddenly reasonable, he'd ask Allison if she still wished to leave. Of course, his wish would be that she says no, but if the answer is indeed yes, then Allison would be returned to her home, finding it nothing more than a house with people she once knew inside it. It was a terrible event that he believed happened to him. It was something that always stuck in his head, but he was almost grateful for it because it showed him how fickle family love is.

If only to understand abandonment, then she would never desire any place but Neverland. He released her and floated up, so he hovered above her like a restless shadow. With a last glance at her sleeping face, he flew from the room and outside of Neverland's atmosphere where the forces in the air seemed exceedingly glad for his departure. As he flew over the ocean, the sun rose then set and the moon copied the sun like it was a competition, over and over, until he saw sight of the mainland. His mind never stopped turning and plotting.

***

Soon as his toes touched the ground of what was Allison's hometown, he ravaged the area until he found an infant that wouldn't be missed. To mothers, he believed, all children are the same and the younger they are the more they are loved and wanted. He held a baby that he had found securely against his chest because he simply didn't have time to look for another in case dropping occurred. Then came the touchy part. He flew to Allison's former home, set the baby on the doorway, and rapped on the door. Quicky after, he flew to the trees to watch Mrs. Joyce find the baby and gather her into her arms. He grinned wickedly and flew to the backside of the house where Allison's bedroom window was.

Carefully pushing it open, he dropped into the room and began ripping all her things off the walls. He opened the dresser, instinctively pulling out a small, strange box. He remembered seeing them being used to take pictures and video during his time looking for Allison. He started pressing buttons until the little screen turned on and a video started playing. There was a man and a little girl who Peter recognized to be Allison. Peter smiled when she smiled and laughed. They were playing in the grass under the tree outside her bedroom window. After a little while of joking around, the man in the video passed a small box to young Allison. She grinned brightly and ripped the wrapping paper then opened the lid of the box. Her eyes sparkled as she lifted a little cross necklace.

"Thank you, Daddy! Thank you, Mommy!" was what she said. A female voice responded but never appeared on camera. The man smiled at the camera. They both said, "Happy Birthday, Alice!" Her smile gleaming and Peter's heart filled with something dark, something close to hate. In one violent motion, he flung the camera out the window and returned to viciously collecting all her things.

With each thing he took, his grin grew wider, and his mind faded to fiction. She was happy then, but something must have happened to make her unhappy now. He remembered how she looked that day, how happy and inviting she had been to him—how easily she allowed him to gather her into his arms. He wouldn't let anything from the mainland hurt her again. He envisioned the future. Each daydream he had, he saw it going his way without any consequence. He imagined waking up with Allison by his side everyday forever and ever. He imagined finally tasting her lips, taking the one kiss that nobody else could have. Then Peter flew all the things out into the woods to be lost. He repeated this until all of her things were stripped from her room and delivered to the middle of the woods. He took the time to dig into the earth and bury it all. It wasn't a perfect job, but it was the best he could manage to do. And just like that, the world she came from no longer remembered her.

Peter returned to the Joyce house. Crouching by the window, he admired the emptiness and lack of Allison's existence in the room. His heart pounded. He imagined that soon there would be a crib in the far corner and toys everywhere. Of course, there would be a rocking chair for Mrs. Joyce to cuddle the infant and sing her to sleep. This could be perfect. Allison would finally understand and be ruined like he had been. He would be everything she ever wanted, ever needed.

Chapter Nineteen

Allison stirred upon Peter's departure from Neverland. It was the stillness that finally woke her. The weight of the place was replaced by unworldly lightness. The treehouse felt undangerous but still wrong. It wasn't just empty—it was hollow in a way she couldn't explain. It had been like that once before, but now it was different. The morning light beamed into the room, high and hot, turning the wooden walls and embedded tree limbs into sheets of pale gold. The side of the bed next to her was cold. The absence stirred her to completely wake. Her tired eyes drifted over the bedroom, finding no trace of Peter.

Slowly, she sat up, her long hair tumbling over her shoulders and framing her face. She listened for a moment. The island was way too quiet. The outer deck of the balcony didn't creak, so he wasn't out there. She threw her legs over the side of the bed, flinching from soreness. She crossed the room cautiously then stepped outside onto the deck that circled the treehouse. She stared at the treetops and the forest stared right back. This time, there were no birds, no wind. The trees stood still, without a single limb swaying and not one leaf waving. In such stillness, you'd think you'd hear the sea roar in the distance, but even that was nonexistent. It was almost like the island ceased living. She shook her head and backed into the bedroom again. Her fingers lingered on the side of the room's entrance wall briefly. The void in the air was so strong it practically had a presence.

Peter was gone. For how long, she didn't know. It surprised her, she thought she'd feel relieved, but she didn't. She sat heavily on the unmade bed again, carefully resting her hands against her knees. They were still too sore to close. It made her recall the other night's chaos. She could still hear the shattering glass, the books bursting like bombs against the walls, pages falling around them like an otherworldly snow. Without thinking, she pressed her palms over her face, wincing from the bruising. She couldn't stand to think of how Benjamin would react if he saw what ruin his hideaway was in. She sniffled, wanting to cry but feeling too empty to do it. Her stomach knotted. She sat for a moment just looking at her hands, her arms. She winced again, but this time it wasn't from physical pain.

She tried not to remember the look in Peter's eyes as he tore the room apart—driven by something too terrible for her to fully recognize. Still, she couldn't help it. Her hands carefully curled then relaxed. With Peter away, she had to find Benjamin. She had to see him and make sure that he was still there…still alive. She pushed herself off the bed without using her hands. Then, she walked across the room to the vanity mirror. She fixed her hair by pulling out the majority of snarls. She sped to the balcony and swung her legs over the rail to climb down. Every move was sore, but she was determined to follow through.

The moment she reached the ground, she looked around. Nobody was in sight. It felt eerie. She stared into the forest, hesitating, scared to go into it alone. She closed her eyes for a moment, hoping and telling herself that she would find Benjamin alive. She forced her feet to go forward.

***

Everything felt so different. There was something that hung in the air, strangely. The sun was bright, illuminating the island. Nothing looked eerie on the surface. It was just a feeling. She moved as quickly as her tired legs could. There was no wind, still not even a peep from a bird. She halted a few times, not wanting to repeat history. She turned and glanced behind her. Still no one. No footsteps following. No shadow darting amongst the trees. It was peaceful, too peaceful for anyone's senses. It made her heart race. It just felt wrong. The trees didn't sway, didn't lean, didn't even breathe. The sun was hot and steady against her skin like the canopy was suddenly nonexistent. It was almost like Neverland was holding its breath in defiance.

She kept walking, quickening her pace. The only sound was the scuffing of her feet against the mossy to dusty ground. The sea still hushed. Out of impulsive curiosity, she veered from the path to find a hill that overlooked the beach. She slowed and stopped. The shoreline was eerily still. The further she stared out, the more the sea looked like a dull silver mirror. The waves weren't crashing. The surface was glass-like and unnaturally calm. She stared down at it, remembered that this was the shore where Will liked to play the most. Her breath hitched and she pushed the memory away. She couldn't think about it right now. Everything was so still, bright, but like death. She had never seen any ocean look like this before, especially not here. She turned quickly, ripping herself from the view. She found her path again, pressing deeper into the forest. She had to find Benjamin. She had to know if he was okay. She moved with purpose but the closer she came to the hideaway she knew was destroyed; she shook.

When she finally reached the clearing, her chest felt tight. The entrance to Benjamin's hideaway was open. The little door at the base of the hollowed tree was just a gaping wound of what was once such a clever shelter. She inched her way to the broken entrance, hesitating at the edge of it. She stared down into the darkness of the tunnel. Her fingers curled into her sore palms. Her throat tightened and body tensed at the thought of what she might find. She forced herself to move down the tunnel. She held her breath slightly as she dropped into the entrance of the room. The ground beneath her feet was cold and uneven, a mess. Then she saw him. Benjamin was sitting on the far side of the room where the bookshelf used to be. His back was pressed against the wall, one knee bent loosely against his chest. His head was also pressed firmly against the wall, his eyes shut. His clothes were streaked with dust. His hair all over the place. His hands were stained with ink. The remnants of his journals and shard glass surrounded him. There were still scattered pages, crumpled and ruined from being walked on. His face was slack, emotionless, but he was breathing—alive.

She exhaled softly. It was a sharp sound in the heavy silence of the room. His eyes flicked up immediately, but when he saw her, his shoulders tensed. His eyes briefly examined her, causing her breath to catch. She crossed the distance slowly, trying not to disturb the pages on the ground. Her heart pulsed in her chest. He didn't look away from her. He didn't speak either. He stayed still. When she finally stood in front of him, she felt unsettled. Almost like she was waiting for him to lash out at her, too. She swallowed and sank down to sit beside him. She mimicked his silence out of reverence. It's not that there was nothing to say, it's just that it was so hard to say the right thing. So, they just sat there. It was hard to see everything she knew he held so dear, all his work and years of writing and recording…all littered across the room.

She opened her mouth to say something, but she couldn't seem to force sound. She knew there was nothing she could do to undo this mess. She couldn't magically piece the journals back together or make up for all of the lost work.

After another moment, she finally forced the words from her mouth, though they were only just above a whisper. "I tried to stop him," Allison said. Her voice was apologetic and hoarser than she expected. She looked at him, but he didn't respond. He just looked toward the entrance of the tunnel, the bottom stair. Benjamin sat there, only moving his hand to the side to trace the corner spine of one of his destroyed books. It was a tender touch, thoughtful, like he was trying to use mentalist powers to soak up the contents of the torn pages before it was too late. Finally, he exhaled and shook his head.

"As did I." His voice was hollow, tinted with grief.

Her chest tightened again. He sounded as if he were speaking through a giant gap in his heart. She scooted closer. His eyes were fixed on the ruined pages in front of them. She hated how his eyes looked now. They were once so full and hopeful but now they were dull and vacant.

Without thinking, she reached out and touched his wrist. "I'm so sorry."

He didn't pull away, but he didn't really acknowledge her touch either. For another long moment, they just sat there, surrounded by the mess.

Then, he spoke. "I'll fix it."

Her brows furrowed, thinking he was referring to the room, the bookshelf, and the journals. She opened her mouth, but he cut her off before she could say something.

"I'll find more dust. We'll gather it again. Together this time, now that I know it is possible," he said.

She stiffened. The words hit her like he had slapped her, but he didn't notice her reaction. His voice slowly had an edge of resolve in it. It felt reckless.

"He's gone now. It's our chance." His eyes met hers, they were filled with eagerness. "We can still get out."

"No." Allison's voice came out sudden and louder than she intended.

Benjamin's expression darkened slightly. His eyes left hers to search for a particular page. When he found it, his hands clenched around it with shaking fists. It was the picture of his father. His voice dropped low.

"You're just scared," he said.

Her face paled. "I am." She didn't try to hide it. "So should you be."

He let out a bitter laugh, short and humorless. "You came this close," he held out his thumb and fingers just barely apart, "and you want to give up?"

She shot up to her feet, giving him a look. "He could've killed you." Her voice broke, but she kept going. "You saw what he did, you saw—"

"And you saw what happens when people stay on this cursed island." He mirrored her by standing, eyes flashing a piece of undeniable truth. "You saw how he handles things."

She flinched from the memories. Her stomach twisted as the flashbacks ripped into her brain. She could still feel the weight of Will's body in her arms, shuddering from knowing that somewhere he was buried in a shallow grave.

She breathed a shaky exhale, and her chest constricted from panic. She shook her head sternly. "Not again. I won't risk it…"

Her voice wavered with a hint of something that made Benjamin close to angry.

"You're so willing to stay." His voice was low with disbelief. "So willing to inevitably die here. Well, I can't, and I won't." His jaw clenched and his hands rounded into fists at his sides. "It will be with or without you."

Her throat closed painfully. She stared at him, her lips parted to argue. She wanted to yell at him that he was being a reckless fool, but the words stuck in her throat. He shook his head and turned away from her, running his fingers through his knotted hair. He paced over the papers on the floor. She watched his steps.

Her voice was quiet, almost like she hadn't yet made up her mind whether she wanted him to hear her or not. "You're being stupid."

He whipped around sharply to face her. "Stupid?" He echoed with the same humorless laugh as before. He gestured broadly at the ruin around him. "Do you not see this? Do you not see what he has done? This is everything I had. It is everything I remembered." He paused, the realization and fear that he had nothing to study, nothing to review, nothing to keep him from forgetting. "And he destroyed it all. Like it was nothing."

Her eyes filled with tears, but he shook his head sharply. "If we stick together, I swear I will not let him destroy us, too."

For a long moment, they just stared at each other. Her chest was tight with panic. Her legs felt weak, almost like she would faint.

"Oh… please," she whispered. "Don't make me."

He noticed the paleness of her skin. He forced his fists to loosen slightly. Then, he stepped closer. His voice was raw with emotion. "I will not leave without you."

She took a long inhale and a slow, deliberate exhale. She shook her head steadily though her legs felt weaker by the second. Her eyes were increasingly glossy with unshed tears. "If that's true," she swallowed, "then you won't leave at all."

Benjamin's face fell, his eyes darkening, which was a look Allison grew to be warry of— usually she only needed to feel that way if it came from Peter. His breathing was so shallow, like he was trying to keep himself controlled. He knew she was scared. The silence was heavy.

"What happened?" His eyes dug into hers. She tilted her head. "What did he do to you that makes you so compliant to stay?"

Her brows knit together. "Nothing."

"I do not believe it," he said, stepping closer when she seemed a little off balance.

She swallowed hard. "It's the truth."

Again, silence filled the space between them. He knew that time was short, whether you believe it or not on this island, time can still be time. With Peter away, this was one of their best moments. Collecting fairy dust is harder to do than you'd think. It was special that she could do it. He needed her. He didn't know what kind of a life he'd have on the mainland. Times have obviously changed. But he believed that there could be something for him. He wanted to change, he wanted to marry, to move forward.

"I have been here for so long. I have seen so much." He told her. Then, he rummaged through the papers on the ground again. Picking up a torn page, he shoved it into Allison's hands. "Do you know her?"

She shook her head, noting the girl's loveliness and Edwardian style.

"I saw her. I never did get involved in any conversation, not like with you," he said. "I stayed far away from everyone at that time, especially Pan."

Allison eyed him. "What are you trying to say?"

"She left him. Her daughter left him. Her daughter's daughter left him…" His voice was distant. He stared at her with purpose. "You are next. This time, I believe something has changed."

She blinked, unsure, but then she put it together. She shook her head in defiance. "That's impossible!"

Benjamin closed a little more distance.

"No. It has been inescapable." He reached her and subtly coaxed her to sit beside him on the floor. She looked at her hands as he kept speaking. "I have never before seen him so aggressive toward a girl. He was never happy to see any of them leave, but he would never make such a fit."

Allison sighed, not knowing quite what to say or what to ask. It all shocked her. "Maybe it'll get better," she said, almost to herself.

"Maybe, but there is another side," he said, his face tight with concern over the shift in the paleness of her skin.

Allison's eyes widened, she barely wanted to hear it, but she didn't have a choice.

"There is a forgetful side. Memories never stay with him, only remnants of things. There is always a fear that if he leaves the island—even if he stays in it—he forgets people. And when he forgets people, a cruel part of him surfaces."

She didn't know what to think. She felt a conflict like she never knew before. A part of her felt sorry for Peter because she did love him. But the other part of her felt afraid. It was so easy for him to do violent things and if Benjamin was right, then what would happen. Peter was gone right now. So, upon his return, would she need to fear him more? The same emptiness that she felt in the morning returned, saturating her. How could she stand to leave? She wanted to, but only on good terms. It was the only right thing to do. She didn't want to risk more anger, more hurt. She wanted to protect the lost boys, at least the ones who were good. She needed time.

"It's not the answer you want, Benjamin, but it's the only answer I have. I need time to think about this. I won't cause any more harm."

His head bowed and his shoulders slumped, but he knew there was nothing more to say. He had to grant her what she wanted. What choice did he have?

***

She used the time to care for Benjamin and other innocent lost boys who were always hiding in different locations on the island in case of Peter's return. Her eyes never stopped looking over her shoulder and she was always listening intently for his crow. The once-green leaves were tinged with a brittle gray, as if Neverland itself was slowly dying without its king. She was more afraid now of what would happen upon his return. The main concern of hers was whether or not Peter would remember her. Whenever she visited Benjamin at their hiding place—a new location now, this concern went unspoken but they both knew by the look on each other's face that they both feared the same thing. Maybe now Peter would be so bored of her that he had forgotten everything and when he returned, she would be killed along with any other lost boy deemed an un-conformer.

Chapter Twenty

But Peter was very unbored. In fact, there was never a time in his total existence when he had been more determined. After moons and moons of travel, he finally came back to Neverland with the loudest crow. The whole island covered its ears, and the smaller parts shuddered and lit the island with adventure in one sudden collective gasp. He didn't need to crow to inform the island of his arrival this time. Everything came to life again as if the island took a deep breath. The wind blew and the treetops shivered. The island cooled and birds rushed around like they woke from a long rejuvenating nap. Even the sea, if you really listened closely, could be heard roaring in the distance. A shudder past through every living creature. As soon as his feet skid against the island ground, he called out for Allison. He flew to the treehouse to look for her, he noted the empty bed, the cold candles. His brows knit, fear gripping him. Flying to the balcony and floating above the roof, he cupped his hands around his mouth and called again, his chest compressing from the force. Nothing. Then he darted into the forest, swift like a winged fox. "Alice!" he cried, shouting as if life depending on making every hair on every creature's body stand on edge.

Peter had been gone from Neverland for so many days. In all that time, she got closer to Benjamin. They shared stories and memories while he scavenged and gathered loose pages, in hopes to put as many things back in order as possible. He tried his best to rewrite whatever was missing. He smiled, appreciating Allison's presence while he wrote. All unbroken things that managed to hide from Peter's rampage had been taken to a different underground room located deeper on the island. Allison was worried that Peter would remember if other hideaways existed, but Benjamin insisted that he'd forgotten them all.

She had been on her way to decorate the new room with wildflowers when the island breathed, a breeze baring a subtle cold-front, which threaded through her hair. She knew he had returned before she could hear his call. She swallowed hard. Feeling it too, Benjamin rushed up from their new hideaway. Closing the door and hurriedly covering it, he almost ran to her side, but something stayed him. She turned to look at him, her eyes telling him not to approach. Benjamin instinctively wanted to beg her to join him beneath the ground where they could plan their escape, but he remembered how she reacted—she wanted time. So, he forced himself to turn around and disappear into the underground room. He no more than closed the door above him when something heavy weighed on his heart. He sat slowly on the third step of the tunnel, his mind unraveling with regret—with all the things Allison still didn't know.

***

As soon as she saw the door of the hideaway shut tight, she turned her attention to the sky, the forest, anywhere where he would suddenly appear. She inhaled and started walking to find the path back to the treehouse. She ran her fingers through her hair, tucking stray strands behind her ears. The last thing she ever wanted to do was cause Peter to suspect. Ducking under a branch, she picked up her speed until she was running. Then, she heard a voice ringing out from up ahead of her. She hurried to reach the voice, knowing it was Peter's. The closer she got, the clearer his voice became until she could tell that it was her name being called. For that moment, there was fear, not for herself but for him. He called for her like something tragic happened. She felt that perhaps he was in danger, so she returned his call by shouting his name, informing him of her location. *He didn't forget,* she thought. He was already floating to the ground. Once he was in her vision and she was in his sight, they ran to each other like a terribly sorry couple who had had their first fight and wanted to right the situation.

She wouldn't openly admit it, she couldn't explain it, but she knew how she felt. The moment Peter returned to the island, the heavy void lifted and something felt right again. She wanted to leave, but there was something about him. The way he could make her feel. She missed how her heart could race, how she truly felt beautiful and wanted. She exhaled when his arms were around her, caging her. She breathed in his scent, like pine and sweet sweat. He squeezed her, burying the side of his face in her hair.

It pained him to say it, though everything was set. "I have been so unfair to you." His voice cracked, his throat tightening.

"Peter," she said, hesitating. She wanted to agree with him, but she was so relieved to have him remember her. She pulled away enough to stare into his eyes. No sign of anger.

"Alice." He pulled her gently to the ground so that they were sitting close together, and he held her hand; "I want you to be glad again. I want you to feel safe. And if going home is what you want, then—"

Her eyes lit up and she tossed her arms around his neck.

"Oh, Peter!" she hugged him, "the lost boys will be so pleased."

It wasn't the answer Peter wished for, but he took a deep breath to ease his increasingly tightening heart and squeezed his eyes shut, inhaling her scent as she hugged him. He allowed her to end the hug first.

"Then, let's get this over with." He said the line more casually than he should have to hide his heartbreak.

"I'll collect the boys!" Allison turned and began to stand to leave but Peter grabbed her.

"No," he said, "Wait to see if you actually like the mainland first. If it is what you want, then I'll bring the lost boys."

Allison didn't like the idea. Perhaps deep down her womanly instincts told her that something was strange, simply too good to be true, but her gladness for Peter's sudden change of heart and her desire to see him as being good, clouded her judgement. She nodded, at this point just wanting to be agreeable. Peter stood and he reached his hand down to her. She looked up into his seemingly dull and patient eyes and took his hand. He pulled her to her feet like she weighed nothing. They returned to the treehouse for what she believed would be her last time.

To remember Neverland, she took her time packing some seashells and pressed-flowers. She gave the treehouse one last glance, then with a heavy heart, they were flying out of the island and beyond its atmosphere. Allison managed a smile when different sights made her feel like everything was a movie. The endlessness of the blue below, the heat of the sun by day and the coldness by night with the gleaming stars to light the path and Peter's warmth all contributed to a distinct feeling. What worried her now was what her mother would say and how she would react. She still felt shame for what she had done on the mainland. There were moments during the flight that made her feel happy. Peter was softer, always keeping a half-smile, but she knew it wasn't from a happy place. She looked into his eyes to search for something that felt unspoken, he would never let it show completely, but it was surfaced enough to stir something within her. There was almost suddenly a sick feeling in her stomach, almost like regret. She wondered how much of his word would be true. She wondered how life could ever be the same. She missed home, but she couldn't quite shake the feeling that happiness might never be felt again. How would she explain her reappearance to her mother. How could she trust Peter's word…how could she say goodbye. Imagine now the lump in her throat when her home was in sight. She held Peter's hand and stepped to the front door, almost ringing the doorbell if Peter hadn't jerked her backward.

"I have a better idea," he smiled charmingly, but inside the smile was a snicker; "Go inside by your bedroom window and sneak into your bed. I bet your mother checks your room each day and would be sweetly surprised to see everything as it once had been."

Allison agreed to this. It seemed a cinematic way to return, so she walked to the back of the house with Peter following close behind. Then, like any proper gentleman would do, he helped her climb the tree so that she could look into her room. She was shaking, but Peter steadied her. As she gazed into the room, Peter watched the excitement fade from her face, a look of total betrayal replacing it. He was right, there was a crib and toys and a rocking chair. Most painful of all was that Mrs. Joyce was sitting in that chair with a new baby girl in her arms. To make the scene worse, Billy's father walked into the room, smiled at Mrs. Joyce, and leaned down to kiss her. Allison gripped her chest and groaned. As he watched tears roll down her cheeks and dampen the corners of her lips, he grew horribly angry, nearly forgetting that this whole scene of total betrayal was his own doing. It was when she started shaking so violently that she might have started pounding on the windows that he gathered her in his arms and carried her far into the woods. She sobbed against his chest and muttered about how much she regretted leaving. But Peter informed her that now she at least knew what kind of a person her mother was.

"You see, Alice, none of them really care." Peter grabbed both of her arms, squeezing slightly when her wide eyes failed to look at him.

Allison shook her head, disbelief pressing her to a new set of sobs. "I can't believe it."

"You don't exist here," Peter cupped the sides of her face. "But you do with me. I'll never forget you, I'll never replace you. You are valuable to me. You may not matter to this world, and no one here misses you, but come back to Neverland, Alice, and I'll make you happy forever."

He caged her in his arms and hugged her tightly. Allison's face contorted with a series of new sobs, but she nodded to Peter and made herself rather childlike so that he would pick her up. It's not very necessary to describe their flight back to the island. All that's important to know is how quiet and gloomy Allison was. This, you would think, would make Peter feel guilty for what he had done but you see, his lie was so close to his own heart and beliefs, that he did only what he knew best to do. He smiled. He would tell Allison about all the fun they would have now and fill her head with how dearly he thought of her.

"Even if I hadn't been replaced," she said during the second night of their flight, "I doubt I would have fit in anymore."

Peter smiled, his heart beating with delight. "That's because you have always belonged with me."

***

By the time they made it to Neverland, and he had tucked her into their cozy treehouse bed, Allison was already choosing to settle. Perhaps, she was being mostly influenced by Peter's own silent feelings about the tragedy of replacement, but such a sudden bubble of resentment burst inside of her. Peter cuddled beside her and lay still, listening to her soft breaths. He imagined how wonderful the days would be. He had won. He couldn't imagine himself any happier until Allison sat up in bed. She was completely silent, and her eyes were unreadable. She swung her legs over the side of the bed, exhaling shakily. There was a sinking feeling inside of him.

"What is it?" he asked, his throat suddenly dry.

But she shook her head and stood up, scuffing her bare feet across the wood plank floor until she paused on the balcony. She crossed her arms and looked out over the dark treetops and all the little fairy homes lit up bright from the glow of each fairy. Peter swallowed roughly, a mixture of fear and dread filling him. He walked, not flew, over to her, standing only a couple inches behind her. Feeling his warmth, she closed her eyes, soaking in the final moments before she got what she wanted off her chest. Then, she turned to face him, her face flushing pink when she noticed just how close he actually was. She opened her mouth to speak but it took a brief moment to gather the right words.

"All my life I've dreamed of places like this," she said. "Then when I finally had it, I wanted to be rid of it and for what?"

Her voice was thick with self-blame, but she didn't look away. She held his gaze, her eyes filled with regret and something even more fragile—the remnants of worn longing, still clinging to some shadow of hope. Peter's brows knit together. His thundering heart almost softening enough to give him a brief desire to tell her the truth. He took a slow breath to deliberately calm himself. He had to remember his plan worked the way he wanted—every piece of it. She was right in front of him, holding the broken parts of her determination in her hands, ready to willingly offer them to him. Yet, there was something that felt like an invisible weight falling around him, mocking his reason and filling him with doubt. She could never fully handle the truth. He has to remember, this is what's best. If he could only have the kiss, then everything would surely be better.

Slowly, he reached out, brushing his fingertips over her shoulder. She leaned into his touch as if she'd been waiting for it, craving it as intensely as he had been. Their eyes locked—her eyes a little desperate now, like they needed to see something that could be proof of something important to her. There was no hesitation in her eyes this time—no uncertainty.

Fireflies appeared and danced in the distance. They began to drift around them, glowing and pulsing softly in the darkness of the treetops like golden heartbeats. The cool night breeze brushed over their skin, carrying the scent of damp earth and sea water. The chill in the air caused her to shiver and she moved closer to him without thinking. She was almost leaning against him, her breath hitching softly, and he felt her release a warm breath against his throat. His self-control twitched, but he didn't move. He told himself that he had to wait. He had to let her make the move. Let her feel like it was her choice only. With a shaky breath and parted lips, she tilted her face upward. He took the opportunity to lean just a little bit closer. The moment she leaned into him, he knew he had won.

Her eyes were a little desperate now. He leaned even closer, deliberately slow. His lips hovered above hers. He hesitated for a split second, almost like he was still willing to give her an opportunity to pull away, decline, but she didn't. At any moment, he expected that she would shy away from him and the chance of receiving her kiss would be gone again, but this moment was different. Allison closed the gap herself. With an inhale, he met her halfway. Her mouth was warm, shy at first. Her breath was slightly uneven from the cool night air, and from everything that was still unsaid between them. She let out a soft, shaky sigh against his lips—barely audible. His eyes closed, already drowning in the sensation.

He gripped her shoulder tighter, pulling her protectively closer to him. It was enough that their chests pressed together, feeling each other breathe. With his other hand, he reached for her face. He cupped her jaw, the warmth of his palm sending a wave across her chilled skin. Her lips slightly trembled, so he steadied them with his own. He moved slowly at first, then deeper—so briefly cautious until it suddenly wasn't. It was a subtle shift. An aching, undeniable turn like one raindrop suddenly transformed into a storm of passion. She made another soft sound against his lips, just a faint hint of a whimper. Something snapped in his chest. His hand fell from her shoulder and wrapped around her waist, tugging her flush against him. He tilted his head, deepening the kiss with hungry urgency. Her hands wrapped around his neck, forcing her onto her tiptoes. Her fingers played with the hair on the back of his head. She clung to him. He could feel her legs weakening, so without breaking the kiss, he caught her hips to steady her against him.

The glow of the fireflies and distant fairy houses flickered. The golden colors blurred around them, making the night feel alive as if the whole island was watching. Her lips parted from his own with a shaky breath. She pulled back slightly, just enough for them to share one more breath. She let her arms fall from his neck so that she could tuck her hair behind her ears though her lips were still brushing against his. Their eyes were heavy-lidded, glazed with want. He almost kissed her again, it's all he wanted now that he had tasted her. But then she spoke, spoiling the chance. She took a moment to catch her breath, making it steady. Her voice was soft and heartbreakingly sincere. It was her tone that made his chest tighten.

"Thank you," she breathed. Her fingers trembled when they reached up to touch his face. She smiled.

Peter's brows narrowed. He had her completely. He would never need to fear again. He knew that he should feel victorious. He did, in a way. But that weight returned the moment his senses returned to normal. Something strangely hollow that clung to the deepest part of his chest seemed to eat at his heart when he looked into her eyes. It frightened him. There shouldn't be anything left to worry about. She was safe... He would ensure it. Still, there was something missing. He leaned in so that his forehead rested against hers and he closed his eyes. Flashes of something blurry and cold pricked his memory as he sucked in her scent and listened to her breathe. He squeezed his eyes a little tighter, trying to force the memories away. They couldn't have him, and he wouldn't let them have her. Never.

Off in the distance, Benjamin hid himself just out of reach from the golden glow spilling down from the treetops. He stared up at them—silent and unseen. His hands curled into tight, aching fists. For so long, he had wished. He had faith and he hoped, but nothing is ever truly that simple. A sharp breath rattled in his chest, but he forced it down, his heart pounding. He fell back against the rough bark of a tree and slipped down in grief. He let his head fall forward, his hair shielding his face as he pressed a trembling fist against the dirt to steady himself. *Hope was a dangerous thing here*, he realized. *It could rot just like anything else.* Through the veil of the trees, he watched Peter lead Allison back toward the treehouse—and it felt like watching a door slam shut forever. From the balcony, the faint glow of fairy lights flickered like dying embers. The forest, alive again with whispers, seemed to lean inward, holding its breath. In the distance, a low rumble of thunder stirred across the horizon—too quiet to startle, but enough to warn.

Change was coming.

And not even Neverland could stay untouched forever.

Here's a sneak peek at

The Never,

the sequel to *The Wish.*

Preface

There's something strange about how some things never truly change. No matter the time, the same stories repeat. This one is no different. The night felt still. It was a kind of stillness that made it hard to concentrate. When there's silence in an aristocratic world, it isn't because of peace, it's because of pressure. James was once the beloved son of a noble family, but now… His heart pounded despite being so torn. He stood there, at the edge of falling from prestige. The sound of his steps bounced off the grand halls of Eton, each echo confirming his fall—each a quiet rebellion. In this society there is legacy or love. For James, he wanted love, but legacy has its own mind. His body tensed as if he could already feel the grand halls rejecting him, the only place he had ever felt a sense of belonging.

Inside a dim room, lit by one flickering candle, she waited for James. The moment he cracked the door open and slid inside the safe blackness of the room (except for the candle), he beheld her. She was beautiful, just as beautiful and intelligent—everything he ever desired in a companion. But just being there with her was reckless. His eyes met her. Her eyes were swollen from crying; her hands, white-knuckled in her lap. He could see the weight of society's judgment on her face. She was everything but this was goodbye. Not because she wanted to leave. Because the world left her with no other choice.

"You know what must be done," she whispered. The kind of whisper that's more breath than sound.

"I can't lose him." James's voice cracked. "I won't let them take him."

"I—I don't know how this happened," she said, stumbling over the words like they hurt to say. "It was never supposed to be like this. A child… It is a scandal. And we cannot survive it."

James clenched his jaw, but a single tear betrayed him. He dropped to his knees in front of her.

"I'll take him. We'll leave. I'll raise him far from all this." He wrapped her shaking hands in his own, warming her cold skin. "Come with us."

She hesitated; pain etched deep into her silence.

"I will never see him again, James."

She stood slowly; her eyes filled with tears she refused to let fall. She picked up the baby from where she kept him sleeping. Her hands lingering over the small bundle for just a moment. She passed the baby into his arms, like handing off something both precious and poisonous. He gazed at his son. So small and innocent, yet already a symbol of all that had been taken from him.

"Promise me you'll love him. That you won't let him grow up feeling like I did. Like he's unwanted."

Her fingers brushed the baby's face, memorizing every line.

"I promise," James said, barely getting the words out past the lump in his throat.

That promise—like most—came with a price. And James paid in full. By morning, his name was gone—burned out of the family tree. He left with nothing but the squirming bundle in his arms. Home didn't exist anymore. Only forward. Only the sea.

***

For a time, James sought solace in small fishing towns. He would leave the baby to his neighbors' compassionate housemaids, begging them to help him while he was away on the open sea. He worked then came back, giving the maids pay. This would continue until the maids' employers discovered the arrangement and put a stop to it. Then, James and the infant would travel to another town. It wasn't until he met Blackbeard that James' destiny as the pirate would surface. Blackbeard—an imposing figure—had heard of James' fall from grace. He didn't ask questions. He just watched James from across taverns and docks like he already knew what kind of man James could become.

"You're running," Blackbeard finally said one night, his voice gruff. "You think the sea can hide you? You think you can outrun the world?"

James had no answer. But something in the pirate's eyes, something bitter and knowing, cracked open the idea of a new kind of life.

James had been hesitant at first, but Blackbeard's words convicted his heart. The sea was infinite, its waves unforgiving, something dangerous. Its cruelness was something he couldn't risk, not with a child—but it was a promise of freedom James had never known. Not in all the years of study, not in all the privileges did he ever once feel free.

With Blackbeard's guidance, James learned the ways and rules of piracy. The ropes, the sails, the endless horizon of ocean—they became his new world. In fact, he was now called James Hook or just Hook because during one raid, he slit a man's throat with an old hook he picked up on impulse. But even as Blackbeard taught him the arts of survival on the high seas, James' heart never left the child. His son, now a toddler, was everything to him—his reason. And he worried about how his son would see him someday. He always kept him safe from the harsh violence of piracy, always told him that they were only fishing or battling whales. But how long could these stories last. Someday, his son would grow old enough to know, old enough to feel shame, old enough to see bad form.

One fateful evening, as the crew of Blackbeard's ship sailed across the misty waters, James overheard a conversation. It sounded at first like a ghost story. He wouldn't have thought much of it, but it was Blackbeard's face that made James take a step forward, joining a conversation that would alter his life forever.

"There's a place," Blackbeard had said, leaning close to James, almost knowingly. "A place no man has ever returned from. Neverland."

"Neverland?" James asked, his voice filled with disbelief. "What kind of place is that?"

Blackbeard's face darkened. "A cursed one. A place ruled by a cruel spirit of youth—a boy who never grows old. Peter Pan, they call him. He'll steal your soul if you let him. Don't go there, James. It's a fool's paradise."

But James could not resist. The promise of a place untouched by time, a place where he could raise his son in peace, seemed too powerful to ignore. With Blackbeard's warning lingering in his mind, he made a terrible decision.

"Maybe I'll find a place for us there," James muttered, the weight of his decision causing even a callous creature like Blackbeard to hang his head.

"You're a fool, James Hook. Mark my words. That island will be your undoing."

Coming soon…

The Never

The island demanded loyalty.

Peter demanded love.

Allison wanted freedom.

And Benjamin—Benjamin found something the

island forgot:

a past with enough power to change everything.

One girl's choice.

One boy's rebellion.

One legend reborn.